Penny Pecorelli has published many articles and short stories over the years and has broadcast on the radio. She lives in England with her Italian husband, but they have a house in Italy which they and their family visit frequently. Penny is passionate about the traditions and culture of Italy. This is her first novel, based on the little hill village in the south of Italy where her husband was born.

For Nonna Maria

Penny Pecorelli

A VILLAGE IN TIME

AUSTIN MACAULEY PUBLISHERS™

LONDON • CAMBRIDGE • NEW YORK • SHARJAH

Copyright © Penny Pecorelli 2024

The right of Penny Pecorelli to be identified as author of this work has been asserted by the author in accordance with sections 77 and 78 of the Copyright, Designs and Patents Act 1988.

All rights reserved. No part of this publication may be reproduced, stored in a retrieval system, or transmitted in any form or by any means, electronic, mechanical, photocopying, recording, or otherwise, without the prior permission of the publishers.

Any person who commits any unauthorised act in relation to this publication may be liable to criminal prosecution and civil claims for damages.

This is a work of fiction. Names, characters, businesses, places, events, locales, and incidents are either the products of the author's imagination or used in a fictitious manner. Any resemblance to actual persons, living or dead, or actual events is purely coincidental.

A CIP catalogue record for this title is available from the British Library.

ISBN 9781035850303 (Paperback)
ISBN 9781035850310 (ePub e-book)

www.austinmacauley.com

First Published 2024
Austin Macauley Publishers Ltd®
1 Canada Square
Canary Wharf
London
E14 5AA

Thank you to my family for their constant support and encouragement. They always believed I would make it someday. Also, of course, to our friends and relations in our own special village who inspired this book.

A special thanks to Eric Carpenter for the incredible cover design.

Chapter 1

"Oh, you idiot!" Sam exclaimed as the enormous watermelon she had been carrying up the steep steps slipped out of her hands and crashed onto the steps below.

It had happened in an instant. One minute she was just about coping with the weight of the huge fruit twice the size of a rugby ball, the next moment a figure had rushed down the steps from above her, shoved her elbow hard, making her stagger and the melon slip from her grasp—and without a word of apology or even a backward glance had run on down the steps and disappeared from view.

What to do? She would have to get another from the market up in the square. Her friend Giulia and her family were waiting for it for lunch. But first of all she had to clear up the mess.

"Rude man," she mouthed to herself as she gazed down despairingly. She had had a glimpse of his back view; tall, dark, slim, dressed in a blue T-shirt and jeans, but she hadn't, of course, seen his face.

She couldn't understand it. She had discovered in the few months she had been in Italy that the Italians were normally the politest, most helpful of people. Even in cities, there was very little drunkenness or bad behaviour and what there was, she regretted to say, was often from foreigners of the type you saw in English towns when the pub turned out on a Saturday night. How could he not have stopped to apologise or even help her clear up?

She made a feeble attempt to push aside some of the melon. She couldn't just leave it or someone would slip on it. Then there was the clattering of hooves from above her. She looked back. It was the old lady who delivered wood with her donkey, scraping a meagre living by collecting wood from the surrounding countryside and delivering it round the village where some people still like to cook on open fires. Usually, it would just have been a part of a charming sight, this old lady and the little grey donkey with branches strapped to his sides. Now it was a lifesaver.

The old lady leading the donkey summed up the problem immediately and with a smile unhooked the spade she was carrying from the donkey's side.

"Posso?" She inquired.

"Of course, you may." Sam said in her best Italian. "Grazie mille. Thank you so much."

Between them they cleared the mess from the steps and shovelled it over the wall onto the bank where at least the birds would have a good feast.

"Grazie," she said again.

She wondered if she should offer to pay, but the old lady said "E niente. It's nothing," and strapping the spade back onto the donkey's side she continued on down the steps.

There was nothing for it but to go back up to the market. She climbed the steps again to the busy market square where stalls were set up once a week and farmers brought their produce, often trekking on foot miles from the surrounding countryside to sell a few eggs or courgettes before trekking those same miles back home again.

The square was a cornucopia of colour and sound; chattering people with their baskets, selecting from the multitude of fruit and vegetables on display; huge red tomatoes, green salad ingredients, courgettes with their yellow flowers still attached, ripe peaches, nectarines, apricots and those curious fruits called Figi d' India, looking like small cacti, but which tasted heavenly once you broke through the spiky carapace. And there was the object of her visit…a huge mountain of watermelons.

"Un altro per piacere, another one please," she said pointing to the one she wanted. The stallholder looked surprised as well he might as she had only bought one half an hour before. He would have recognised her anyway. There weren't many English girls wandering around small villages in the south of Italy and she was an object of curiosity to all the locals.

"Un altro?"

"Si." She didn't have enough Italian to explain what had happened.

She paid, picked up the watermelon and hugging it to her like a precious baby, made her way carefully through the chattering crowds in the square and back down the steps, praying that this one would reach home safely.

She had been living in Naples for the past few months, helping her uncle in his art gallery. He had invited her over when she finished her three years at art college and she had jumped at the chance. He had introduced her to some of his Italian friends and Giulia, the daughter of one of them, had invited her to spend a few days with her family in her village in the mountains some twenty miles outside the city. Her uncle had said, "Of course, take as long as you want. It's good for you to see as much of Italy as you can and village life is especially interesting with the old traditions still very much alive."

So, she had arrived after a torturous journey along winding mountain roads and precipitous hairpin bends at this enchanting twelfth century village set high on a hilltop in the midst of a wooded valley. Stone houses, their walls keeping out the winter cold and the heat of summer, were perched precariously on the sides of the hill, their narrow windows and balconies looking out over the dramatic drop into the valley below. On the very pinnacle stood the old Church of San Nicola, the bell tolling every hour even through the night.

Giulia had explained that villages were built like this to protect them from warring bands and the French, the Greeks and even the Etruscans had been part of the village's history since mediaeval times.

For Sam it was enchanting. She had wandered around exploring every nook and cranny, soon discovering that most of the inhabitants, even some of the most elderly, were far fitter than she was due to a lifetime of climbing the steep stone steps. The only vehicles allowed in the village square at the top were those delivering goods. Everyone else had to park at the foot of the hill and walk.

It was a maze of tiny narrow streets and easy to get lost. On almost every corner was a tiny shop of some kind; a grocer's frontage hung with huge globular cheeses, strings of onions and garlic, legs of cured ham, baskets of lemons, the leaves still attached to them. Inside the tiny cavernous rooms crammed with goods, the often elderly shopkeepers sometimes had an even older relative dozing in the corner, waking now and again to ask for a drink or something to eat before nodding off again. There was a cobbler's shop, the man himself with a mouthful of nails, sitting hammering a sole onto a shoe that was resting on his leather apron. There were shops full of bed linen and clothes, often full of aprons and overalls for the working man rather than the latest fashion from Milan, she noticed with amusement. There was also a little convenience shop which sold a myriad varieties of pasta and tins of tomatoes for the ubiquitous tomato sauce.

Now as she made her way back to Giulia's house, she admired the wrought iron balconies filled with pots of bright geraniums. Others on the far side were lined with washing. If you were careless when you were attaching your pegs it was more than dangerous. Drop a sock here, Sam realised, and it would never be seen again, plunging hundreds of feet down into the valley below. Cats stalked on terracotta roofs or lay sunning themselves on the hot tiles. Little backyards were filled with rows of vegetables and perhaps a lemon or orange tree. Hardly an inch of space was wasted. It was warm, but cooler here than in the city and Sam knew that many people escaped here in the summer from the stifling heat of August. There was a small hotel on the road below converted out of an old palazzo and many people arrived in the summer months. Tourists came to admire the frescoes in the old Abbey of San Antonio in the valley and revel in a simpler way of life before they returned to their often frenetic lives.

She arrived at Giulia's house at last and went up the steps and through the front door. The kitchen was at the back of the house and she went along the hallway and placed the melon with a thankful sigh onto the table.

"You were a long time," Giulia remarked in her almost perfect English, "did you get lost?"

Sam explained what had happened.

Giulia frowned. "Who was it who hit you?" She queried.

"I don't know. I didn't see his face. A man, quite young looking, but he was hurrying away so I only saw his back view."

"How rude," Giulia said, "it must have been a visitor. It doesn't sound like something anyone in the village would do."

"That's what I thought," Sam said.

"Che successo?" Giulia's mother Maria was asking what had happened. Giulia explained and her mother was suitably horrified. She was a nicely rounded middle-aged lady with her hair pushed up in a bun and a lovely twinkle in her eye. Sam had taken to her immediately. They fussed over her, plying her with a cool drink and made her sit down as if some terrible catastrophe had occurred.

Once settled and refreshed, Sam watched as Maria expertly mixed and rolled the pasta dough for lunch then cut it into tiny strips before wiping her forehead with a floury hand. Giulia was alternately grating the Parmesan cheese and stirring the pot of fresh tomato sauce simmering on the stove. A pan of water stood at a rolling boil and Maria added a dollop of oil and a good pinch of salt.

"The oil is so the pasta doesn't stick together," Giulia explained.

Sam gazed around her at the old wooden dresser that had probably sat there for generations, at the assortment of mostly unmatched colourful china, at the stone walls which had stood the test of time and were crowded with black and white and sepia photos of past generations all gazing sternly into the lens of the camera; at the table itself, scrubbed by those same generations of women, where a vast platter of salami and ham and baskets of bread stood waiting. In the short time she had been in Italy she realised that bread was very much the staff of life, plenty of it at every meal. From where she sat, she could see the balcony overlooking the rushing river below, with lines hung with freshly washed bed linen, some of it no doubt trimmed with handmade lace from Maria's trousseau many years before.

Nothing about the scene before her was in the least bit up-to-date or modern, but it was comfortable, homely and vastly reassuring.

Her reverie was interrupted by Maria's call. "Cinque minuti, a tavola tutti quanti." Five minutes to lunch, the call for everyone to sit down. The table had been cleared and a cloth laid out together with water, wine, knives and forks, glasses and plates.

As if by magic, Giulia's two younger brothers Tommaso and Giovanni, 13 and 15, both tall and bright-eyed, appeared from the bedroom where they were supposed to be doing their homework, but were probably playing a game on their computer. Then the front door opened and Giulia's tall grey-haired father Enrico entered. He was the mayor of the village and worked in the council offices in the main square. In fact, the whole family were loyal to their roots as Giulia was a teacher in the little primary school at the bottom of the hill.

"Ciao Sam," Giulia's father bent to kiss her on both cheeks before taking his accustomed place at the head of the table and pouring himself a glass of the local wine. Sam couldn't imagine her own father in England drinking wine with lunch every day, but she knew Enrico would probably have a small siesta before returning to his desk in the square.

Giulia passed the steaming bowls of pasta ladled out by her mother and everyone helped themselves to Parmesan and bread. After the events of the morning, Sam realised she was very hungry and set to eagerly.

She was suddenly aware that the eyes of the boys were fixed on her as she ate. Maria said something sharply to them in Italian. Sam looked inquiringly at Giulia who went slightly pink.

"They are watching you eating the pasta," she explained. "My mother told them it was rude to stare, but you are doing ok. Most English people I have seen down in Naples cut it up into small pieces with a knife and fork, but you've learnt the proper Italian way of twirling a few strands with the fork prongs down on the dish."

Sam laughed. "It was the first thing my uncle taught me when I arrived, how to eat pasta properly. He said exactly the same things about the tourists." She smiled at the boys who both had the grace to look down and concentrate on their food, suitably chastised.

After the huge bowls of pasta had been consumed, the remaining tomato sauce wiped clean with chunks of bread, they ate the home-cured salami, ham and some provolone cheese and finally, the watermelon cut into huge slices which the boys delighted in holding up, pretending they were huge pink smiles reaching to their ears.

Sam sat back with a satisfied sigh. "Please tell your mother that that was the best meal I've ever eaten and thank her."

Giulia did just that and Maria received the compliment with a smile of thanks. The boys immediately disappeared and Maria and Giulia cleared up, ignoring Sam's offer of help. Sam looked forward to the day when she would be treated as part of the family and not as a guest and would be allowed to help. Then the adults sat with their small cups of espresso coffee.

Just as they were finishing there was a commotion at the door, a frantic knocking. Giulia went to answer it. One of the neighbours stood there gabbling excitedly. The only word Sam could understand was 'medico', doctor and 'ambulanza' ambulance. Obviously, something serious had occurred to disturb the peaceful atmosphere of the village. Sam sat frustrated at not being able to comprehend what was going on.

Eventually Giulia translated. It seemed that old Paolo, one of the shopkeepers, had had a heart attack and the village doctor was nowhere to be found, but a visiting doctor from Naples had heard the urgent plea for help and went to stabilise him before the ambulance had made its torturous way up the hairpin bends from the nearby town. The doctor's prompt action had no doubt saved old Paolo's life and he was, it seemed, the hero of the hour and there was a gathering in the square to give thanks where he was being showered with drinks and compliments.

"Come on," Giulia said, "let's go and see what's happening."

They raced up the steps to the main square where the market stalls had been cleared away and in their place was a huge crowd of people. It seemed that a large spontaneous party was going on, the babble of voices rising to a crescendo. Someone had even started playing the accordion. Sam smiled.

Any minute now, she thought, there would be dancing. She had soon learnt that in Italy there was any excuse, however slight, for a party.

Giulia pulled her through the crowds to the centre and there, suddenly, she saw a figure facing away from her. There was something familiar about his back view, young, black hair, jeans and a blue t-shirt.

She gasped in fury.

"What is it?" Giulia asked.

"You know I told you I was almost knocked over by someone, why I dropped the melon? That's him. I'm going to have a word with that young man and tell him exactly what I think of him."

"No, wait," Giulia called urgently, but Sam was determined.

She pushed her way forward through the crowd and confronted him. He smiled at her politely.

"Do you speak English?" She demanded, hands on hips.

His expression changed from one of polite interest to a frown as he looked at her angry face.

"Yes, I do," he confirmed "Why?"

"Good, because I want to ask you why you nearly knocked me off my feet this morning without even stopping to apologise. I could have fallen down the steps you pushed me so hard."

"I...I," the young man stuttered, his expression changing again.

"Well?" Sam said, her voice rising even more indignantly. "What have you got to say for yourself? Is that the way you normally treat women?"

"I'm sorry," he replied stiffly. "I didn't realise. I was in a hurry. I do beg your pardon."

Sam suddenly realised Giulia was beside her, touching her arm. "Sam listen to me."

But Sam interrupted. "This is the very rude young man I was telling you about."

"Sam!" Giulia was nearly shouting at her now and there was a silent crowd around them, listening eagerly to what was going on.

"Sam," Giulia said, more gently now. "This is my cousin Federico. He is a doctor in Naples and I've just found out that it was him who saved old Paolo's life this morning. I think he must have heard someone calling for a doctor and rushed to help. That's why when he cannoned into you he didn't have time to stop and apologise. It was an emergency."

Sam went scarlet with embarrassment and for a moment was speechless. She took a deep breath.

"Oh," was all she could say eventually. "I'm so sorry, I quite understand. I...I." She stood miserably, tears pricking at her eyes. She had made such a fool of herself, without knowing the facts. Still, she thought defiantly, how was she to know?

The crowd around them had grown even bigger now, staring at her. Mostly, she realised, because they were speaking English. There was a muttered murmur of whispers as those who understood English translated for those who didn't. She heard the word 'l'inglesina', the English girl, mentioned. Of course, she thought ruefully, it had to be a foreigner causing all the fuss.

Without looking at him again she turned and fought her way back to the balustrade overlooking the valley, gazing out with eyes half obscured with tears.

After a few minutes, Giulia joined her and put her arms around her. "Come and talk to Federico. He wants to apologise properly."

"Oh, Giulia, I feel so stupid; and with everyone watching, when they were all praising him as a hero too."

"You weren't to know," Giulia said, "and he must have given you quite a fright when he ran into you."

Sam turned round and Federico stood there. In any other circumstances, she would have been rather impressed by what she saw. A serious expression, but devastatingly good-looking, a long lean figure, a mass of dark hair, an aquiline nose and surprisingly dark blue eyes.

She realised she was staring so she tore her eyes away and looked down at the ground.

"I really do apologise," he said, "I would never normally behave like that, but all I could think of was getting to a seriously ill patient."

"Yes, yes, of course, and I apologise for shouting at you. I didn't know the facts."

"Friends?" He said, reaching out to take her hand in his and smiling.

She took his hand in hers and it felt suddenly so comforting. He must be such a kind and reassuring doctor, she thought, he has such a lovely manner. They stood for a moment still holding hands, both reluctant it seemed to be the first to withdraw.

"Come," Giulia said finally to Federico. "We haven't seen you in ages. My mother will be delighted to entertain you again."

She and Federico walked down the steps chatting together, with Sam trailing miserably behind. What must he think of her? She realised suddenly with a shock of recognition that she cared very much what he thought of her. How could that be when she had only just met him?

The conversation when they arrived at Giulia's house was voluble and sadly, to Sam, almost incomprehensible. Even if she had known more Italian, a lot of what they were saying was in the local dialect which she knew Giulia lapsed into when she was at home, rather than proper Italian.

Maria had thrown her arms around Federico and hugged him. Giulia explained that Federico was the son of Maria's brother who had sadly died many years before so he was especially dear to her mother.

Cantucci were produced, those sweet almond biscuits, and dipped into Vin Santo, sweet Italian wine, together with cups of coffee.

Finally, Federico turned to Sam and said "Tell me, why do you have a boy's name?"

"Oh," Sam said, "it's short for Samantha."

"Samantha," the way he pronounced it was delightful, each syllable stressed, "that is a lovely name and you shouldn't shorten it."

It turned out that he had taken a few days off to stay in the village in his old family home and catch up with his relatives. He had only just arrived when he heard the shopkeeper's daughter screaming for help, desperate for a doctor.

21

"Never off duty," he said ruefully. "That's the trouble with my profession."

He left finally, promising to come back for lunch the next day. Sam found herself already looking forward to that time.

"He's nice," she said to Giulia, trying to make her voice sound casual, but her heart was beating fast.

"Yes, he'll be quite a catch for someone. Sadly he's already taken. I've never met her, but I think there's a long-term girlfriend somewhere in Naples."

Sam's heart lurched and she was amazed at how devastated she felt all of a sudden.

Chapter 2

The following morning was a Sunday and Giulia and her family went to early mass. Sam elected not to go as she wasn't a Catholic.

She picked up the little sketchbook she took everywhere with her and set off to walk around the village once more. She eventually found herself right at the foot of the hill in the valley where the river ran. She walked along the bank, weaving her way through clumps of wild flowers, trying not to tread on the colourful blossoms, watching the birds dart from tree to tree in search of insects and listening to the sound of them singing. It was glorious and she took a deep breath to fill her lungs with the pure mountain air. She loved the hustle and bustle of city life, but she also loved being away from the constant traffic noise and the din that constituted life in Naples. She finally settled on a convenient tree stump at the water's edge. She leant forward to trail her hand in the fast-flowing current, enjoying the rush of the water as it raced towards the sea. Then, as she leant further forward she found herself slightly over balancing. Her whole arm went in and the side of her dress was soaked. The shock of the cold water made her gasp.

Feeling slightly foolish she straightened up, glad that no one was around to see her.

Suddenly a voice came from behind her. "At least it wasn't my fault that time."

She whirled around.

Federico was standing behind her. She hadn't seen him coming through the trees.

"Oh, buongiorno, good morning," she stammered.

"Sorry, did I startle you?"

Sam smoothed down the wet side of her dress as much as she could, acutely conscious of his eyes on her. The dress was clinging to her waist and hips. She couldn't help but hope that he liked what he saw.

"May I?" He indicated the log.

"Of course."

He sat down beside her and there was silence for a moment. Then he said, "I love coming here, so peaceful and quiet after the chaos of the city. When I was studying for my exams it was my favourite place to, how you say…unwind?"

"I can see that," Sam replied. Then she asked, "What kind of a doctor are you? I mean, do you specialise?"

"I am training to be a cardiologist."

"Well, it seems you are a good one if the events of yesterday are anything to go by. How is he by the way? Have you heard?"

"I rang last night and it seems he is out of danger. He will make a full recovery."

"Thanks to you," she smiled.

"He is fortunate I was around. He would have died otherwise."

She could see he wasn't boasting, just stating a matter of fact.

He asked her about her life in Naples and what she was doing at the art gallery.

She explained how much she enjoyed her job and how she hoped to do some of her own art as well when she had time.

"It must be wonderful," he said, "to be surrounded by beautiful things all the time."

"Oh it is," she said enthusiastically, "I am so lucky. And I love living in Italy as well."

"I'm glad. I do too." He laughed and she smiled back.

There was a brief silence, and then he continued "Look at those chestnut trees. They remind me of a story my father told me about my grandmother and her sister-in-law. You have to understand that people of my grandfather's generation got married very young. My grandmother and her sister-in-law were both only sixteen, still young girls really."

His face was animated as he remembered the story and she had trouble resisting the urge to reach out and touch his cheek.

"Well," he continued, "they went out one day to gather chestnuts. It seemed that each thought the other had brought something to put them in, but neither of them had."

Sam waited as he paused for the punch line. "What on earth were they to do? Finally they decided that the only solution was to take off their knickers…they still wore those heavy ones with elastic round the legs…tie them up and put the chestnuts in them."

He was grinning as he recounted the tale. "So they arrived home and they were spanked by their respective husbands for their unseemly behaviour."

"I love it," Sam laughed. He was very near her on the log, almost near enough to feel his heart beating. She didn't want this moment of closeness to end.

Then he said, "Have you explored much round here? Herculaneum? Pompeii?"

"Neither." Sam replied. "Not yet."

"Oh you must go; they are fascinating."

She thought for a wild moment that he was offering to take her, but then he continued, "You must get Giulia to take you."

He made to get up. "And you must get back and change out of that wet dress."

He was grinning.

"Absolutely," Sam said. "Well, it's been fun chatting to you."

"Yes, well, goodbye. I'll see you at lunchtime." She hoped he was going to lean forward and kiss her cheek, but, after a moment's hesitation, he turned abruptly on his heels and walked away.

As she gazed after him her feelings were in turmoil. She had never quite believed in the concept of love at first sight, that proverbial coupe de foudre, a clap of thunder, but she was definitely, quite definitely experiencing it now.

The trouble was that if he already had a long-standing girlfriend it was quite obviously useless, utterly useless.

She wandered back up the hill, suddenly feeling very despondent.

"What in earth happened to you?" Giulia exclaimed looking at her drenched state.

"I went down to the river to do some sketching and I sort of overbalanced."

"Good job you brought a change of clothes then," grinned Giulia. "If you must try and go swimming with your dress on."

Federico arrived at lunchtime. "Hello," he said, "you look a bit drier than the last time I saw you."

Giulia looked at Sam. "Oh, you've already seen each other this morning?"

Sam explained that they'd bumped into each other earlier down by the river and had a brief chat. She found herself blushing, "I made an idiot of myself yet again." She attempted to make a joke of it, but the humiliation of the day before was still fresh in her mind and she tried not to meet Federico's gaze.

"Not at all," he said reassuringly. "Falling in the river can happen to anyone. I did it all the time when I was young."

She looked at him and he was grinning.

They sat at the kitchen table and Maria produced another fabulous meal, but Sam found herself for once strangely lacking in appetite. She was acutely aware of him sitting next to her. Space was tight at the kitchen table, so several times his arm brushed hers and at one point they reached across for the oil at the same time and their hands touched.

After lunch he chatted briefly with the family, answering their questions about his life in Naples. "Mostly work and sleep," he said ruefully. They didn't ask about his social life and no girlfriend was mentioned, but Maria asked if his mother was keeping well. He answered that she was, but Sam wondered about the slightly reserved tone in Maria's voice. There was no warmth in her query and no offer to send her regards or best wishes. She was intrigued, but no doubt Giulia would enlighten her later.

"You must take Sam to Pompeii sometime," he said to Giulia.

"I plan to," she replied. "It's top of my list."

After coffee, he made his apologies. "If you'll excuse me, I have some work to do, some case notes I need to check. I must go back to the house. Thank you for lunch. It was good to see you all again." He hugged Maria and Giulia, shook hands with Enrico, and said, "Ciao" to the boys then, as if on an afterthought, turned to Sam and kissed her briefly on both cheeks "Goodbye, Sam, I hope we meet again. I must come and visit the gallery sometime."

"Please do," Sam replied. "It would be lovely to see you."

And with a final farewell to everyone, he was gone.

Chapter 3

The following day he had gone, back to his busy job in the hospital.

The day after that, Sam herself bade farewell to the family in the village and Giulia drove her back to Naples, leaving her outside her uncle's gallery. She left, but not before making Sam promise that she would return to the village soon, a promise that Sam was more than happy to keep.

Sam really loved living with her uncle Richard 'above the shop' as it were. The apartment was spacious with an enormous kitchen and a flower-filled wrought iron balcony where they took breakfast in the morning gazing out at the wonderful panorama of the Bay of Naples, its sparkling blue sea dotted with bobbing boats. At twilight, they had supper there, eating shellfish that had come straight from the sea that morning; lobster, prawns and crab, together with pasta with mussels or clams. Richard, her uncle, loved to tear the shellfish by hand, picking out the delicate meat and eating it with mayonnaise and freshly picked lemons bought from the market that morning. She had quickly learnt that he was, to use the modern expression, a foodie. Eating was his number one passion.

Richard, her mother's brother, had left England long ago to settle in Italy. He lived with his long-term partner Gianfranco. Richard was short and portly, now white-haired and partially bald while Gianfranco was tall and skinny with jet-black hair which Sam suspected had more than a little help from a bottle.

They made a wonderful couple, affectionate with each other and with her, always laughing and teasing. Gianfranco was the cook, concocting delicious dishes, humming along to the opera music he played constantly and sometimes more than that, singing lustily. She grew used to sudden bursts of Nessun Dorma or O Sole Mio. If the truth be told he had a pretty terrible voice, but if he enjoyed it who was she to complain?

She had her own large bedroom on the far side of the apartment and thought she had died and gone to heaven when she opened the wooden shutters in the morning to see the view of the bay and the street scene below where a passing youth might look up and shout "Ciao Bella" and blow her a kiss.

And the uncles, for it was easier to think of them in the plural, would spoil her; oh how they would spoil her!

"Nice to have someone to spoil," Richard would say when he persuaded her to buy the shoes she had stopped to admire in the window of a nearby shop; which he would then pay for.

She soon learnt not to admire things too much or they would appear as if by magic at the breakfast table the next morning. He had learnt the Italian way of generosity and hospitality.

They took her to the markets, especially the one in the Forcella district, the old historic heart of Naples, rich in history and tradition. They introduced her to the best pizzas.

"This is where the pizza was invented," Gianfranco told her, "made in proper wood-fired pizza ovens."

And ice cream, gelato, to die for. Nothing like some of the watery versions she had had in England, but rich and creamy and in so many different flavours it was almost impossible to choose. She was also introduced to granita, a kind of water ice, really refreshing on a hot day.

Richard explained to her that before Italy was united in the nineteenth century, Naples was part of the Kingdom of the two Sicilies, an independent state with a king and a palace at Caserta. "We'll take you there one day," he said. "It's spectacular."

The people too were amazing, full of verve and cheek. They weren't on the whole as sophisticated as she had heard people from cities like Rome or Milan were. She had never been to either, but she knew there were huge differences between the north and the south of the country. Here there were always abundant smiles and everyone seemed always happy. Perhaps the climate had a lot to do with the way people behaved.

"After all," Richard said, "who wants to live in a place like Milan which is covered in fog for three months of the year?"

"Exactly, caro mio," Gianfranco had agreed. He of course always called Richard 'Ricardo' and Richard had laughed when Sam had said how much nicer it sounded in Italian than in English.

"Ah Sam, beware," he said making her giggle. "Just remember that if you are out with Tommaso, Ricardo and Enrico you are only ever out with any old Tom, Dick or Harry."

One thing though she did have to sort out fairly quickly was her wardrobe. Because she had been a student for three years, most of it consisted of t-shirts, baggy jumpers and jeans. After college she had taken any old job she could find to earn some money and had hoped to travel for a year before settling down to a career. She considered teaching, which would have meant more studying, but what she really wanted to do was to produce her own artwork. The chances of actually making any money out of her painting though were so slim as to be infinitesimal, but a telephone conversation at Christmas between her mother and uncle led to the best Christmas present she could have imagined in her wildest dreams, the offer of a job in Richard's gallery.

Italy, the land of Michelangelo, Caravaggio, Leonardo. What could be more wonderful? Aside from helping in the gallery, she hoped that she could do some sketching and painting of her own. When her mother had told her what Richard had proposed, that she come out to Italy and see if she enjoyed working with him, she had nearly been suffocated by the ecstatic hug from her daughter and her squeals of excitement had her father running in from the garden thinking there was a fire.

So there she was, in the job of her dreams, but still looking like a student. She saved her next two months' salary carefully and then with an afternoon to spare she set forth determinedly. The trouble was where to go? She dared not venture into the designer shops on Via Chiaia, the Italian equivalent of Bond Street, but she did window shop to get an idea of the styles that were fashionable. Her figure was good. What she needed were a few smart basics that she could wear every day in the gallery. She envied the Italian girls who emerged from the sea in a bikini with wet hair and then came out of a beach hut ten minutes later looking like a visiting film star. They all seemed to have a natural grace and poise that most English girls didn't possess. Sam felt positively gauche in comparison.

She soon learnt that in Italy there was hardly ever such a thing as a badly designed dress. Even the cheapest garments were stylish so she traipsed from shop to shop, often eyeing the other, Italian, customers, noting anything that looked particularly good. And, of course, she didn't tell the uncles what she was doing or they would have wanted to buy everything for her. They did however notice how smart she looked and complimented her on her appearance the first time she appeared in one of her new outfits, a chic black trouser suit.

She loved working in the gallery, mixing with the artists who came and went and helping with the parties the uncles gave on the opening nights of exhibitions. Richard was the expert framer of the two and she soon learnt how the cut and attach simple frames for prints and insert the glass. It was Richard's task though to do the more elaborate framing for the more precious pictures in oil and water colour.

Gianfranco on the other hand was skilled in restoring pictures, meticulously cleaning every inch with tiny brushes to reveal the beauty underneath. The results were usually spectacular and they would all stand admiring not only Gianfranco's work but also that of some long-dead painter whose artistry had long been obscured by grime and neglect. It was all so satisfying being surrounded by art all the time.

If ever things were quiet she sat with her Italian grammar, trying hard to learn as much as possible as quickly as possible. It was a lovely language, so musical, the language of love and of opera, but she found it very hard to pronounce and she also soon learnt there was a very strong local dialect in Naples which made things even more complicated. Luckily, most of the people who came into the gallery spoke English and there was always an uncle around if things got complicated.

One day in the early evening while she was out exploring she passed the hospital San Gennaro, the main hospital of Naples, where she knew Federico worked and she wondered if she would ever see him again. Then she shook herself, telling herself not to be so foolish. It was all a pipe dream. He would never ever look at her in that way.

Then one day the door of the gallery opened and in he walked.

It took her a moment to realise who it was because the sun was behind him.

After the initial shock, she collected herself and smiled. "Federico how lovely to see you again," she said as coolly as she could.

He came forward and kissed her politely on both cheeks, gripping her hands as he did so.

"Samantha, good to see you too," he said politely.

He released her hands and then Sam realised he was not alone.

He turned to the figure next to him, a tall elegant blonde young woman dressed in the finest that the designer shops of Via Chiaia could offer. "Sam," he said, "may I introduce you to my friend Nadia. Nadia this is Samantha or Sam as she likes to be called, my cousin Giulia's English friend."

"Piacere. How do you do?" Nadia said politely.

And looking at the beautiful, elegant, sophisticated figure standing before her, Sam realised that whatever silly dreams she may have had about Federico, she didn't stand a chance, not in a chance in the world, of capturing his heart.

Chapter 4

You could not fail to be moved, Sam thought, as she gazed down at the writhing figures frozen in time when Vesuvius spewed out its molten lava over the citizens of Pompeii. She had seen those images so many times on television back in England, but to see them close up, their hands twisted in their last plea for life was quite another thing. Two thousand people had died in Pompeii itself, but many thousands more in the surrounding countryside. She had been surprised at the size of the site as it sat under the snow-capped volcano which loomed menacingly over the Roman city. "Many people think before they come here that it is only a village," Giulia said, "but you can see how vast it is." Indeed it had taken them hours to wander through, marvelling at the villas richly decorated with frescoes, amazingly preserved despite the metres of ash which had rained down on them on that fateful day in 79AD. There were three of them wandering through the complex and Sam hadn't been able to suppress a little jump of surprise and pleasure which she had tried hard to conceal when Federico announced that he would be accompanying them.

"I haven't been for about ten years," he said by way of explanation, "so it will be interesting to see what further excavations they have done in that time." It had taken them about an hour to drive from Naples after they had picked Federico up from outside the hospital. On the way Sam had gazed up at Vesuvius dominating the skyline.

"They say that the citizens of Pompeii didn't realise it was a volcano until it started to steam." Federico said from the back. He had kindly let the girls sit in front and was sitting behind Sam who was in the passenger seat and she was acutely conscious that he must be studying the back of her neck.

"Can it still erupt?" She asked nervously.

"Possibly," he replied. "It has erupted several times since Pompeii, but they keep a pretty close eye on it. Mostly there is just a bit of steam that comes out occasionally. You can go up there if you like. They take you by bus to the bottom then you walk to the top. It takes about an hour to climb to the edge of the crater."

"Think I might pass on that one." Sam laughed.

"There's what they call the Red Zone at the base, the real danger area," he continued, "with quite a few towns and villages that would be in the line of fire, but the burning ash could actually reach Naples if the explosion was big enough."

"Fingers crossed then that they are monitoring it properly," Sam said with a shudder.

"But there's also a very special wine made from grapes grown on the slopes," Giulia interjected, "It's called Lacryma Christi, the tears of Christ. We must try it sometime. Accidenti! Whoa!" She had braked sharply as some idiot on a Vespa had cut her up. She muttered a rude word, then said, "Sorry, Sam."

"No, don't apologise," Sam laughed. "It all adds to my vocabulary."

If it was crowded on the roads in Naples, it wasn't much better when they left the city. Theoretically the roads were faster, but they were often clogged with the little battered three-wheelers the farmers used to deliver their goods.

"They're called Apes with the accent on the e as if it were an a," Giulia explained.

"Isn't that Italian for bee?" Sam asked. "I suppose they buzz…like the scooters are Vespas 'wasps'?"

"Well done, you're learning fast." She swore again as the car in front of her stopped abruptly without warning. Everyone drove so close together. Sam privately thought she would never be able to drive here, but if she stayed maybe she would have to eventually. If she stayed. It depended on a lot of things. One of them was the person sitting right behind her.

"It's not only the traffic," Federico said, interrupting her thoughts. "I have a friend who once, when he had just learnt to drive, borrowed his mother's car for a jaunt in the mountains. She wasn't too keen and had made him promise to be careful, but of course, being young and foolish, he was driving too fast and went round a corner smack into a wild boar."

"Accidenti!" Giulia said again, overtaking another Ape. "What happened?"

"Well, as you can imagine he was pretty shaken and worried about the damage and what his mother would say, but he got out to look at the dead boar and the car which, he was relieved to see, wasn't too badly dented." He paused.

"Go on," chorused the girls simultaneously, "What happened next?"

"Well he had a bright idea. His mother could make a whole load of pasta sauce and salami out of a wild boar, so he hauled it up and slung it in the back seat; with difficulty as they are huge animals. He drove on whistling happily, thinking that his mother would forgive him the dent when she saw the boar."

"So was she pleased?" Giulia asked.

"What happened is that," Federico started to laugh and they had to wait until he collected himself, "is that the boar joined him in the passenger seat of the car."

"What! Madonna!" Giulia nearly lost control of the car.

"It was only concussed, not dead. So you can imagine it was pretty upset at finding itself on the back seat of a car being taken home for sausages."

"So what did he do? Your friend I mean?" Sam asked.

"He bailed out as quickly as possible and locked the car while the boar rampaged inside trying furiously to get out and destroying the whole interior of the car in the process."

"Mamma Mia," Giulia said, "I'll bet his mother had a few words to say about that."

"I think he's still paying off the debt," Federico laughed. "Though the fact that they did in the end have to shoot the boar meant that his mother got her salami, so he was partially forgiven."

They had still been laughing when they arrived at Pompeii but then, looking down at those tragic figures their mood had changed abruptly. After that, they visited the enormous amphitheatre with its serried semi-circular rows of stone seats. They stood at the very top, what would have been the upper circle in a modern theatre.

"It's enormous," Sam breathed. "How did anyone at the top hear what was going on? They didn't have loudspeakers in those days did they?"

"Wait," said Federico as he lightly skipped down the steps of the aisle to stand where the actors would have been thousands of years before. "Ciao Samantha, come stai? How are you? Mi senti? Can you hear me?" Sam was startled. His voice came loud and clear.

"That's amazing," she said to Giulia. "I can't believe it."

"You'd better believe it," Federico said, because of course he could hear her as well. He bounded back up the steps to join them.

"They still hold concerts here," Giulia said. "All the Roman and Greek amphitheatres are like it. They were built in such a way that they had natural acoustics. Go to any of them and you won't find a loudspeaker anywhere."

They moved on to the forum, the market square, with its huge impressive pillars where the citizens of Pompeii used to meet on their daily business. Sam could only imagine the passeggiata, the daily walk that Italians still take every evening where the population came out after the day's work was over to catch up with their neighbours and exchange news. It brought it home to her that these were living, breathing people, much like themselves.

"The archaeologists even found jars of preserves and calcified bread loaves." Federico said, which made them even more human in Sam's eyes. They passed through the basilica, used as a courtroom, and admired the wonderful frescoes in the Temple of Apollo. There were shops and public baths, temples and many private houses. It was vast. Federico was waxing more and more lyrical. He was so enthusiastic about showing her everything and she could feel herself becoming more and more besotted with him by the minute. He held her hand to steady her as they crossed the enormous rutted roads with the high stepping stones across the centre that acted as a sort of zebra crossing and once or twice she caught him looking at her and then looking away abruptly as he met her gaze. Then once, determinedly, she caught his look and held it. She smiled and, after a pause, he smiled back.

Something in that moment really meant something, something unspoken, but deeply felt.

They arrived at the House of the Tragic Poet. "This is my favourite of all the houses here," he said, his face lighting up. "Not the biggest, but it is the most interesting. Look, it says Cave Canum on the door."

"Beware of the dog," laughed Sam. She felt intoxicated with emotion at being near him at that moment. "So that's where it comes from. He looks more like a wolf."

The floor of the house was covered with wonderful mosaics and the walls with frescoes depicting scenes from Greek mythology. "It's wonderful," breathed Sam, "but why is he the tragic poet? I mean tragic I understand because he died in the eruption, but how do you know he was a poet?"

"A lot of the artefacts from Pompeii have been taken to the museum in Naples, but there is a mosaic of a man sitting reading so he looks like a poet reading his poetry. They even found the shell of a tortoise he must have kept as a pet." They reached a building called the Lupinar.

"What's this?" Sam asked.

"Look up," said Giulia with a grin. "Guess!"

Above the main door and each doorway as they wandered through… and it took a moment to register…was an erotic picture. Some of them were very explicit indeed. She suddenly realised that the strange diagrams they had seen everywhere throughout the whole site were in fact phallic symbols. She blushed.

"Lupinar means the wolf den," Giulia explained. "A lupo is a wolf and the prostitutes were called she-wolves."

Sam was acutely conscious of Federico standing next to her. She tried not to catch his eye.

He smiled wryly.

"I think the phallic symbols are meant to bring good luck. The tintinnabula were penises hung with bells as wind chimes." He said it all matter-of-factly, but of course he was a doctor so he would be very matter of fact about the human body, thought Sam.

It got worse. There was a statue with a huge erect phallus and yet another. Had she just been with Giulia they would have no doubt giggled like a pair of school girls, but with Federico standing alongside her she felt herself going scarlet. She hoped that they thought it was just the heat. Then, when she accidentally brushed his arm it was worse. A tremor shot through her and she fought hard for self-control. It was almost a relief when they finally left Pompeii and climbed into the car for the drive home. She thanked heavens that Giulia was there as she tried desperately to sound normal as she made small talk with Federico, but she was relieved when they finally got back to Naples. They stopped in front of the gallery and he said he was happy to walk back to his flat.

Giulia drove away after making Sam promise to come to the village as soon as she could. Federico leant forward and for a wild moment she thought he was going to kiss her on the mouth, but instead, he kissed her politely on both cheeks. But he did hold her hands in his and, perhaps she imagined it, yet again he held them for a fraction longer than was strictly necessary. He turned and walked away and she gazed after him, her heart beating fast. He reached the corner and just as she thought he would be out of sight, he turned and looked back at her. He half raised his hand in salutation and smiled. She raised her hand in reply.

Then he was gone. It had been such a wonderful day. They had got on so well. Why would he have come today if he wasn't at least a bit interested in her? It wasn't just that he wanted to see Pompeii again, surely? But then again, she thought, this is all a pipe dream. Images of him standing next to Nadia, that tall elegant figure with her arm through his, flashed through her mind.

The uncles were out and the flat was empty for which she was profoundly grateful. Her mind was in turmoil as she reached the cool of her room and threw herself on her bed.

"Damn, damn, damn." She muttered to herself. "This is ridiculous. I am being ridiculous. I need to get a grip on myself and stop being so silly. He is merely being kind."

Or was he? Was there some hope? After all, he wasn't married yet.

She really didn't know.

Chapter 5

Business was slow so Gianfranco suggested that she should first of all deliver a package to one of their long-standing clients and then perhaps take the rest of the morning off to explore.

"You're sure?" Sam was delighted. She raced upstairs and changed into t-shirt and jeans. She picked up the parcel and set off through the streets of Naples, deftly avoiding the cars, trucks and Vespas which seemed to have a Highway Code all of their own. She had to remind herself frequently that traffic drove on the opposite side of the road in Italy to that in England, but not necessarily in Naples where it seemed to be a free-for-all and on no side in particular.

It wasn't far to where their client lived, in an apartment on the top floor of an old palazzo that had seen better days, but which still had an air of faded grandeur.

She pressed the buzzer for the apartment she wanted, entered the dim hallway and took the ancient lift, with its clanging wrought iron gates, which then creaked and groaned its way to the top floor.

She rang the bell and after a very long wait the door was opened by an equally creaking old retainer who led her into the drawing room of the spacious apartment where their client, the Contessa, sat regally ensconced on an antique gilt chair, dressed in a long sweeping velvet gown with diamonds at her ears and throat. She was perfectly made up with hair freshly coiffed, but still Sam could tell she was probably even older than the creaking retainer.

Sam knew there were many such people of noble lineage, titles descended from the days before Italian unification when this had been the Kingdom of the two Sicilies. Confronted with the elegance of her hostess and her surroundings, she wished she hadn't changed into her t-shirt and jeans before visiting and felt slightly uncomfortable in the presence of the Contessa who, despite her grandeur, was obviously delighted to have some company, isolated as she was in her ivory tower in her old age.

She was offered coffee which came in a fine porcelain cup with a crested silver tea spoon and they made conversation, or what passed for it, despite Sam's poor Italian and the Contessa's broken English. While they spoke, Sam gazed around her discretely at the photos of high society massed on exquisite little gilt tables which recorded the glamorous life the Contessa had led. Above Sam's head were glittering Murano glass chandeliers and beneath her feet were faded antique Persian rugs. Heavily framed portraits, presumably of the Contessa's noble ancestors, lined the walls and the curtains were of silk, faded long ago like their owner. She handed over the package she was delivering which unwrapped with trembling hands, duly admired and passed to the creaking container.

At last, she was able to bid the Contessa a polite goodbye and she made her way downstairs again by way of the clanging lift. She went through the dimly lit hallway and finally opened the huge wooden door of the palazzo and stepped out into the sunlight.

"Ciao Sam," came a surprised voice behind her.

She whirled around.

It was Federico.

"What are you doing here?" He asked.

"Oh hello, I was just delivering a watercolour that we had framed, to the Contessa on the top floor." Sam explained. "And you?"

He gazed at her. "I've just come off duty and I was on my way home. It's been a long night."

Indeed, Sam thought. He did look very tired and careworn.

There was a brief silence and then he said, "Shall we walk together?"

"That would be nice," Sam replied, her heart fluttering.

They walked down to the sea-front, the Lungomare. Then he said, "I'm starving."

He looked at her. "Would you like something to eat? I haven't had breakfast yet."

"No, I'm fine," Sam replied, "but you go ahead. I'll sit with you."

They found a cafe on the seafront and sat in the sunshine. Sam watched in amusement as he devoured a huge ciabatta roll stuffed with salami and downed two cups of double espresso.

He sat back, replete.

"Ice cream?" He said. "Surely you won't refuse an ice cream?"

"No, that would be lovely," Sam replied.

He ordered from the waiter and after a few minutes, two bowls of luscious-looking vanilla ice cream arrived, together with two more coffees.

"Wow," Sam said. "You will be hyper."

"I need the caffeine," he smiled, "to keep me awake."

"Sorry if I'm sending you to sleep."

"No, no, it's not that. It's just that I've been on duty for twelve hours straight without the chance to even sit down. Anyway, one of the coffees is for you."

"Oh thanks," Sam said. She went to pick it up, but he stopped her.

"Ah, no, wait," he said.

He leant forward and she watched in surprise as he picked up the coffee and poured it over her ice cream. Then did the same with his own.

"It's called Affogato," he explained "Drowned icecream."

Amused, she picked up her spoon and tried it. It was delicious. She tried another spoonful.

"Sometimes you can add grappa or even brandy, but I thought that was a step too far for this time of day. I might fall forward flat on my face into the ice cream and be sound asleep."

She laughed.

"It was my father's favourite," he said wistfully. "He always poured the coffee over the ice cream with a flourish."

There was a pause.

"How long ago did your father die?" She asked at last.

"I was nine. He was ill for two years and they tried everything to save him." He was looking down as he spoke, struggling with his emotions. Even though it was many years ago he obviously still felt the pain of the loss acutely.

"That must have been so hard for you," she said gently.

"The worst thing was not knowing what was going on. People think that because you are a child you shouldn't be told things, but it makes it worse because you can see someone getting weaker and weaker and turning a dreadful colour, but everyone is trying to be cheerful when you are around and telling you everything is going to be alright. Then when he died they didn't talk about him with me. My mother shut herself away and hardly spoke to me, or every time she did try she started crying and nothing I could do would comfort her. So I began to feel it was my fault."

He looked up at her with an agonised expression.

Sam spontaneously reached over, took his hand and held it. They sat in silence only broken at last by the bells of the nearby church chiming the hour.

"Sorry," he said at last. "I must be overtired. I don't know where all that came from. I've never said anything like that before to anyone," he said, looking at her face. Then he said, "you are so easy to talk to."

"Don't be sorry," Sam replied. "It needed to be said. Was that why you decided to become a doctor?"

"Yes, yes, I suppose partly that. But I think I would have become one anyway because that was what my father was."

"And your stepfather?"

"He's a lawyer. He's a nice enough man, but we don't have much in common. My mother married him when I was thirteen and he tried his best. I suppose that's a difficult age anyway. I used to do so much with my father, boat trips, fishing trips, hikes in the mountains; but my stepfather isn't interested in any of that. Still he seems to make my mother happy enough so I guess that's the important thing."

He broke off and made an effort to smile.

"I think I have complained long enough. I apologise if I've sounded sorry for myself. I am not really. Some people have much harder things to cope with."

"No, no, don't apologise." She stopped; then she plunged in, "I hope this is not too intrusive, but will you show me your father's old house the next time you go to the village? I know you stay there sometimes."

He looked at her in surprise, "I'd love to," he said. "Thank you. It would give me great pleasure to show it to you. Mind you, it's not very grand, just a simple village house and rather neglected," he confessed. "I just don't have the time to update it. But then I suppose I like it the way it is because it is full of memories of him."

Then he tried to stifle a yawn "Sorry," he said, "but I really must go and get some sleep."

"But of course," she said "and thank you for the…what did you call it?"

"Affogato."

"Ah, I must remember that. I'm sure my uncles will have heard of it."

"Bye Sam," he said, bending to kiss her on both cheeks. "And thank you for listening to me droning on."

Then he turned and walked away, unsteady with exhaustion and she gazed after him, hopelessly, helplessly in love.

Chapter 6

Total bliss, Sam thought, to be sitting under a vine-covered pergola in Italy on a June day with a table spread before her and surrounded by lovely people all chatting away.

They were on the farm in the valley where Giulia's family had been invited for lunch by Enrico's elder sister Philomena. Her name translated as 'nightingale'.

How lovely, Sam mused. And that was exactly what she was like, a small bird, tiny and wiry and full of energy. She had been bustling about, preparing huge mounds of food. Sam could see them now, she and her daughter in the kitchen making the pasta. This time it was little pieces of dough broken off and pressed expertly with their thumbs into small shapes.

"Orecchiette," said Giulia, "like little ears." Which is exactly what they looked like.

There were at least twenty people at the table ranging from an elderly great uncle to the tiniest of Philomena's great-granddaughters sitting in a high chair and undisputedly in command of all she surveyed. Not for the first time did Sam think that in Italy the bambino, or in this case, the bambina was king or queen, kissed frequently, spoilt rotten, cuddled often and generally adored. They were indulged, certainly, and to English eyes, they might seem unruly, but they were secure in the knowledge that everyone in the family loved them and they grew in turn to be affectionate and outgoing adults.

Huge carafes of homemade wine appeared, wine pressed on the huge wooden structure that Sam could see in the corner of the barn. The vineyard was small but come September, Giulia explained, they would all come to help pick the grapes and press them.

"With your feet?" Sam asked jokingly.

"Of course," Giulia laughed. "No, sometimes people do it for fun, but we do have a very efficient machine now. I hope you will be here to help. It's a hard day, but a good one. The grapes have to be picked and pressed on the same day so as not to waste any of the juice."

Philomena's daughter was cutting huge swathes of the local bread, clutching the traditional huge round loaf on her bosom and cutting towards herself in the way that Maria did and which always made her wince. The slices were then piled high in the centre of the table, plenty of it because as usual, a meal without bread in Italy was unthinkable. There were flasks of extra virgin olive oil, also from the olive trees on the farm. Giulia explained that when the olives were ripe Philomena's husband supervised the spreading of the nets and the boys were sent up the olive trees to shake the branches so they didn't lose any of the fruit. Then it was taken to the local press with its huge grindstones to have the oil extracted and bottled. Bread was eaten always by dipping it in oil.

"It's only in the north that they use butter," Giulia went on. "That's why we are all healthier down in the south," she grinned. "My aunt and uncle are very, how do you say in English?"

"Self-sufficient?" Sam suggested.

"Yes, yes, that is the word. They buy very little food. They have pigs and chickens and also goats for milk. They make their own salami and cured ham. They bottle and preserve fruit and vegetables and Philomena makes endless jars of tomato sauce from their own tomatoes. You will see that everything we have today the family have prepared themselves."

True to her word, huge piles of sliced prosciutto and salami appeared on the table with bruschette, plates of toasted bread piled with minced liver or fresh tomato.

"Don't eat too much," Giulia warned her. "There are a lot more courses to come."

"Yes I think I have come to understand Italian hospitality." Sam laughed. "You are pressed to eat until you feel sick, but you dare not refuse for fear of offending your hosts."

She was still laughing when she looked up…and there was Federico appearing suddenly at the kitchen door.

A cheer went up as several people rushed to embrace him.

"Mi scusi, I am sorry," he apologised. "I was kept late on duty at the hospital by an emergency."

"No problem, sit, sit, eat," came a chorus from all around the table.

A large glass of wine was poured for him and he removed his jacket and rolled up the sleeves of his shirt as he sat down. He was four spaces up from Sam on the other side of the table. He raised his glass in salutation to everyone and as he did so his eyes lighted upon Sam. He nodded and she smiled back.

Did she imagine it or did his hand tremble, making the wine shake?

Wishful thinking, she told herself.

He gathered himself together and continued toasting everyone around the table before taking a sip of the wine and then helping himself to bread and salami. Sam concentrated on not letting the tomatoes fall onto the front of her t-shirt from the bruschetta and then she looked up to see that Federico was watching her. Their eyes locked for a brief moment and he smiled that devastating smile that made her heart turn over.

She smiled in return, then concentrated hastily on catching a piece of tomato as it escaped from the toast and stained the front of her t-shirt. When she looked up again he was grinning. Once more she was looking foolish in his eyes. She was mortified as she hastily dabbed at the stain with her napkin.

Eventually, when every scrap of ham, salami and bruschetta was eaten, Philomena and her daughter rose from the table and went back to the kitchen. Giulia's uncle and the two sons also rose.

"Can we help?" Sam whispered to Giulia.

"No, no. I think the kitchen is Philomena's domain; and the men have gone to feed the pigs. It will be a while until the next course. Shall we walk round?"

The children were eagerly running round the yard and Giulia and Sam also left their seats. As they wandered Sam noticed a hutch full of rabbits busily eating lettuce and pieces of cabbage. The girls admired the enormous neat vegetable garden full of tomatoes, beans, lettuce, artichokes, and almost any kind of fruit or vegetable you could think of, plus a fig tree, a walnut, a cherry, a lemon tree and an orange tree.

Philomena's daughter Teresa came to pick some fresh lemons. Then they stood for a while watching the men feed the pigs and Sam bent over and scratched the back of the nearest porker.

"They like that," came a voice next to her. She glanced sideways, startled. Giulia had moved away to talk to one of her cousins and Federico was by her side.

She smiled nervously, her heart jumping.

"I enjoyed our trip to Pompeii," she said eventually.

"Yes, it was good," he agreed. After a pause, he said "We must do it again sometime. I mean, not Pompeii again, but somewhere else. There is so much else to show you."

"I'd like that," she replied, then added, "very much."

His hand touched hers briefly and she almost gasped at the pleasure she felt.

They were interrupted by a voice calling. "A tavola tutti quanti, everyone back to the table."

She sat next to Giulia again and he returned to his place four spaces away and began to talk to his neighbour. Steaming bowls of the orecchiette were produced, drenched in tomato sauce, doled out of an enormous saucepan. Everyone helped themselves to Parmesan and they tucked in. One of the teenage grandchildren was watching her closely and she wondered if, like Giulia's brothers, he was watching her eating pasta, but he said curiously, "Are you really English?"

"Yes," she said, "I am. Are you learning English at school?"

"Yes and I would like to come to England to learn more."

"We have special summer schools in England. Maybe when you are older your parents will allow you to travel there."

"I would like that," he said. "Then maybe I could also go to some concerts. Then maybe also I could meet Ed Sheeran."

Sam laughed. "Maybe, but I can't promise that."

Sam promised him that they would talk more in English so he could practice. His face lit up and she smiled. She was acutely aware of Federico watching her from the other side of the table and she blushed as he nodded approvingly at the sight of her conversing with the young teenager.

Pasta finished, bowls were wiped energetically with bread to ensure that not a scrap of sauce had been missed. They all rose from the table again, apart from a few elderly relatives who remained to chat although Sam noticed that two of them were already contentedly napping.

This time it was the spectacle of the goats being milked that Giulia led her to. The young boy accompanied them, trying out his English eagerly at everything they passed, with Sam encouraging him.

The eldest son of the farm was leaning his face against the flank of the nanny goat, expertly directly the jet of milk into a bucket. In the meantime, the grandchildren were up in the branches of the cherry tree supposedly picking the fruit for dessert, but Sam noted to her amusement that there were more cherries stuffed into mouths than put into the wicker basket below. She suspected that there would be more than one case of tummy ache that night judging by the cherry-stained mouths, and the amount of pips they were dropping down below.

Philomena and Teresa had of course once again disappeared into the kitchen and it was a longer than usual wait for the call of "A tavola!" When they eventually sat down again Sam noticed that it was already after three o'clock and she suspected that they wouldn't have finished the meal much before six.

They sat down to huge plates of chicken, together with zucchini flowers stuffed with ricotta cheese, grilled aubergines, pickled artichokes, bowls of fresh lettuce and slices of huge beefsteak tomatoes. Oil and balsamic vinegar were liberally sprinkled. Despite Giulia's warning about eating too much, Sam had found everything so delicious she had already overindulged, but she managed a bowl of salad and a few pieces of chicken, in between translating for the teenager who doggedly pestered her to keep teaching him English. She realised that the rest of the table was listening attentively to her English lesson and there were a few people loudly repeating what she was saying. She noticed too that he and the other grandchildren, apart from the very smallest, were allowed a little wine, heavily watered down.

"You have a very clever grandson," she assured Philomena. "His English is good."

Philomena smiled with pleasure and patted his head, "Bravo, bravissimo," she said before enclosing him in a bear hug which, despite her small frame, Sam could see was surprisingly strong. Embarrassed in true teenage fashion he struggled free, but Sam could see he was pleased. The rest of the table echoed "Bravo," and Sam could see Federico joining in. He nodded at her approvingly again and mouthed "Well done."

They rose once again from the table. This time they went to see the chickens being fed with all the scraps from the kitchen.

"I can see life never stops on a farm even when you have guests for lunch." Sam laughed.

"Quite," Giulia agreed.

They were passing the rabbit hutch and Sam was surprised to find there were no rabbits inside. Then she suddenly realised why. It wasn't chicken that they had been eating, but rabbit.

"Oh," she said.

Giulia looked at her startled face. "I told you that the food here was very fresh," she said wryly.

"Well," said Sam reluctantly, "I'm not used to eating rabbit, but," she conceded, "they were delicious."

Federico was still talking to one of his cousins. They were in animated conversation and Sam, when they returned to the table was disappointed when he didn't look at her. The cheese was produced, an enormous whole pecorino made from sheep's milk, then Philomena presented them with a wonderful dessert with sweet cake drenched in liqueur, chocolate and custard, rather like a trifle.

"Zuppa inglese," Giulia explained, "in your honour."

"English soup." Sam laughed.

"Grazie Philomena," she said and Philomena accepted the thanks gracefully.

It was delicious and nothing like a soup.

By the time they had finished, the sun was dropping lower in the sky. Sam couldn't believe that even now more food was being produced. Bowls of ripe peaches and apricots, what was left of the cherries that the grandchildren hadn't eaten, all followed by strong espresso, glasses of Strega, Grappa and Limoncello.

Conversation was slower now as everyone was replete. In fact, there were now more people nodding off than before. Even Sam herself was feeling rather sleepy and her eyelids were drooping when she heard a car crunching over the gravel on the farm track.

Federico rose from the table. "1 must go," he said as he gathered up his jacket. He went round the table saying his goodbyes, kissing everyone affectionately on both cheeks. He came at last to Sam and she felt his breath on her face as he kissed her in the same way as the rest.

He saved a special hug for Philomena, then he went round the house to the front yard. She could see an Alpha Romeo waiting there. Inside was Nadia.

He climbed in beside her and Sam could see clearly that he leant forward to kiss her; not on the cheeks, but on the lips.

It was as if someone had kicked her in the stomach. She felt sick. She had thought he had been encouraging her, that there was a chance of a relationship. In fact, all he had been doing was playing fast and loose with her feelings. Fury assailed her. If that was what he was like, playing around with more than one woman, she didn't want anything more to do with him. He was, in old-fashioned terms, a cad.

"How dare he, how dare he!" She raged to herself. She felt tears springing in her eyes and she fought hard to prevent them spilling over.

"What is it?" Giulia asked solicitously "Are you alright?"

"Nothing, nothing. I think the wine has gone to my head; and too much sun."

Then she thought to herself '*I must pull myself together. He hasn't actually been leading me on at all. He has just been attentive and friendly and perhaps mildly flirtatious and I am overthinking the whole thing in a stupid immature way like a schoolgirl.*'

But however much she scolded herself for her emotions the sun indeed had gone from that wonderful day and it was all utterly, utterly spoilt.

Chapter 7

Sam could smell the appetising odour coming from the kitchen in the house that quickly had become so familiar to her.

"What's for lunch today?"

"Choke the priests." Giulia laughed.

"What?" Sam was shocked.

"Strozzapreti," Giulia explained. "It's a kind of pasta which means 'choke the priests', little twisted strips."

"How did it get that name?"

They were standing in the hall side by side gazing at their joint reflection in the mirror.

"I think it comes from when there was a lot of resentment about wealthy, greedy priests and the women would make that sort of pasta in the hope that the priests would choke when they ate it."

"Great," Sam said, "and I thought Italians were really nice people!"

"You know," Giulia was looking at the pair of them in the mirror, "no one would think I was a typical Italian, or what people think of as typical Italian: short, round like my mother, pale skin, freckles, auburn hair. Whereas you, tall, slim, long dark hair, brown eyes; if they had to guess which one of us it was they would always choose you. Are you sure you don't have any Italian blood?"

"Not as far as I know," Sam laughed. "Pure Norfolk through and through. Maybe someone came over with the Romans a long time ago. All I know is that I feel very at home here, very happy in Italy, so maybe I do have roots here."

"I'm glad," Giulia hugged her.

"I hope your mother doesn't mind me being here so often."

"Mind? She loves it. She sees we are good friends and also it's great for the boys because you are helping them with their English. Their teachers are amazed at how much they have progressed recently. I think that English before you came was just another boring school subject, but now they realise that people actually speak like that and understand it and it has given them a whole new perspective."

"Good," Sam said. "I am happy to help them in any way I can."

"Anyway, they can now understand all the lyrics of the English and American pop songs they love which is an added bonus." Giulia laughed. She paused. "I was going to ask you that if the uncles can spare you, could you come into the school sometimes and help me teach the little ones some English? They can never start too young. I'm always aware that I have an accent and perhaps don't always put the words in the right order, so it would be good for them to listen to you."

"Of course, it would be a pleasure," Sam replied. Then she continued. "I never asked you where you learnt your English. I know you spent some time in England which is why your English is so good, but where were you?"

"Bury St Edmunds. I went there as part of my teacher training. The college thought it was important that I learn English."

"So you weren't that far from me all that time. How strange."

She hesitated. "I wanted to ask you about your cousin Federico. He has never actually lived in the village?"

"No, he just comes back sometimes to stay in his grandparent's house which was left empty when they died. He came back particularly when he was studying for his medical degree to get a bit of peace and quiet."

"I know, he told me."

"Really? Oh?" Giulia gazed at her but didn't comment. "Anyway, his father was from the village, my mother's brother Vincenzo. He went to Naples to study when he was young, met Federico's mother Olivia and they settled in Naples. That's why, although Federico comes here from time to time some people don't recognise him. My mother was devastated when her brother died quite young and she didn't even know he was ill. His wife didn't even have the decency to tell her."

"I can only imagine," Sam sympathised. She realised why there had been an edge to Maria's voice when she had asked Federico about his mother.

"I still remember the time even though I was only young," Giulia continued. "As you know, funerals are arranged very quickly in Italy. They are often the next day, and instead of being buried here in the village in the family tomb which he should have been, Olivia insisted he be buried down in Naples so she could visit the grave more easily. I suppose it was her right to do that, he was her husband, but my mother was dreadfully upset and they haven't had much contact since. I shouldn't say this, but she seems quite a cold woman, from some sort of aristocratic family and she gives herself a lot of airs and graces."

She gazed at Sam curiously, "Why do you ask?"

"Oh, no reason really. I just wondered about his background, if he actually spent some time here."

"Yes, of course, my mother and her brother were brought up here and when their parents died my mother was already married to my father and didn't need the house so she gave it to Federico. I think she thought it would encourage him to visit more often."

"That was kind of her."

Giulia shrugged. "Yes, of course, but it meant that she could hang on to the family connection and seeing him sometimes would be a link to the brother she had lost. She doesn't talk about him that often but I think they were very close and losing him was incredibly painful."

"It must have been."

"But why did you ask? Are you interested in him?"

Despite herself, Sam couldn't help blushing and Giulia gazed at her friend.

"Oh no, no more than I am interested in all your relatives," Sam protested, but Giulia wasn't convinced. She had the good sense though to keep quiet and privately thought that she was very sorry for her friend if that was the way the land lay. She had never met Federico's girlfriend as he had never brought her to the village, but she had heard that it was a long-standing attachment since childhood.

"Right," she said, changing the subject abruptly, "time we went into the kitchen and got to grips with those choking priests."

"Absolutely," Sam replied, "I'm ravenous."

Chapter 8

Sam gazed out at the sea of upturned faces in front of her. All the small children were dressed in their smocks with huge white pussycat bows, blue for boys and pink for girls. Sam wondered if modern children in England would tolerate such a uniform, but the tradition died hard in Italy.

It was a delightful sight and she envied Giulia her job teaching small children, though she knew it brought its own stresses and strains and was not always idyllic. There were a dozen children from the village itself and half a dozen more from surrounding villages.

The gallery was closed on Sunday and Monday so luckily she was able to stay over several times a month and visit the school on Monday mornings with Giulia. She had at first prepared a few topics to talk about, but she had soon learnt that children were unpredictable in their eagerness to learn and most of her notes were ignored.

On her first day, she had been unaccountably nervous, especially because of her imperfect Italian, but she soon relaxed as the barrage began. She had started by asking, "Do any of you know any words in English?"

A hand shot up "Football," shouted a small boy, "Arsenal, Manchester United, Liverpool, Chelsea."

"Very good." Sam laughed. "Anyone else?"

A little girl raised her hand timidly. "Queen Elizabeth, Princess Kate, Princess Charlotte, Prince Carlo."

"Good," Sam said, "though we say Charles, not Carlo in English. Can you say, Charles?"

"Char…less," they all chorused.

"Yes, well done, though he's King Charles now. King Charles the third. This means the third king called Charles."

And so the lesson had progressed, with Giulia sometimes stepping in when Sam had difficulty translating, but they all learnt to ask, "How are you?" and "I am very well thank you."

Then the little boy who had put his hand up first asked how to tell the score in football so they worked on their numbers.

"How do you say niente?" He asked.

"That could be 'nothing' or 'nil'."

"So, Italy fifteen and England nil," he said hopefully and everyone, including Sam, laughed at his cheek.

She was asked if it always rained in England and did people carry umbrellas all the time. They seemed surprised when she said no, that sometimes it was as hot as Italy, but not as often and in England it was usually greener because of the rain.

They asked about English children and if they went to school in the same way and did they wear uniforms? Sam told them that English children sometimes wore a jacket and tie to school.

"What like grown-ups?"

They were impressed.

"My father has been to England," said one little girl importantly and everyone turned to look at her. "He has been to Glasgow and Cardiff."

Sam didn't correct her geography, but asked if they watched any English films on TV and it turned out they all loved Peppa Pig and if they ever came to England that is where they would like to go first, to Peppa Pig World.

"Thank you, Sam," Giulia had said after their first session. "That was wonderful. Will you come again soon?"

"Of course," Sam said. "As often as I can. That was fun."

So, over the next few months, Sam went to the school quite often. She was gratified that the children's faces lit up when they saw her and she was glad of the distraction from her thoughts about Federico. She had branched out into art lessons, teaching them to sketch everyday objects which of course included using the English words as each object or animal was described.

One lovely day when it was too hot and stuffy to stay in the classroom, Giulia decided that they would take the children down by the river in the valley. The children were of course delighted and wanted to run ahead, but Giulia took them firmly in hand. She was at the front of the little crocodile while Sam took up the rear, helping little Alfredo who wore callipers on his legs, probably due to a hip displacement, and who had difficulty keeping up with the rest on the rough ground. It was hard for him. Because of his disability he often felt left out of things, but that day he was delighted because he had Sam all to himself and he kept a tight hold of her hand. He was a bright, endearing little boy who never complained and although Giulia had confessed that as a teacher you should never have favourites, he was secretly one of them and Sam had to agree.

"Your teacher looks like the Pied Piper," Sam laughed looking at Giulia leading the line of children. Alfredo looked puzzled.

"The story of the man who took the children away because the town wouldn't pay him for getting rid of the rats," Sam explained.

"Ah," his face lit up, "Pifferaio Magico!"

"Is that what he's called?"

"But she's not going to take us away," he said matter-of-factly.

"No, no, of course not."

"I wish I could speak more English," he said.

"You will soon learn. Anyway you know a lot of English already and you don't realise it."

"I don't."

"Yes, yes you do. What is spaghetti in English?"

"I don't know."

"Yes, you do. It's spaghetti. We say the same."

"Really?" He grinned. "And pasta? Lasagne, fettuccini, linguini all of those?"

"Exactly… and Macaroni, cannelloni."

"And Pizza?" He said hopefully.

"Yes and mozarella, cappuccino, gelato, panino."

So they played a game using all the Italian words that Sam could think of that were used in English and it distracted him from the struggle to get down over the uneven ground. "You see we like Italian things so much in England that we haven't bothered to change their names."

"That's cool," he said, beaming.

She helped him over the last big rock and they arrived at the river where Giulia had already tried, with difficulty, to settle the children with their notebooks. Several of the boys wanted to go in the water, but Giulia could be surprisingly strict when she wanted to be and they eventually did as they were told, still grumbling.

Sam showed them different things they could draw. "Flow...ers," they chanted and the different colours, plants and trees they could see. They were soon drawing busily while Sam answered queries on the words they wanted translated.

Peace descended apart from the odd giggle and slight scuffle about borrowed pencils, but as Sam gazed around her she couldn't help but remember that first magical morning when she had come down to that idyllic spot and how she and Federico had sat on the log together. She recalled how embarrassed she had felt with her wet dress and the memory of how she had shouted at him when she had confronted him that first time in the square. The nuts on the chestnut tree he had talked about were ripening fast and she smiled, remembering the story about his grandmother.

She was interrupted from her reverie by a burst of laughter. Alfredo was boasting to all his friends how he knew a lot of English words like spaghetti, lasagne, cannelloni and so on. For once he didn't feel left out, but the most important person there and Giulia looked over to Sam and mouthed, "Well done" and put her thumb up.

....

What Sam hadn't realised was that Federico had been watching from up the hill as the little school party wound its way back at the end of the morning's session.

Sam looked up and saw him standing gazing down at them and her heart leapt with delight.

She was holding Alfredo's hand and trying to help him over the uneven ground, but it was much worse going up than coming down and he was really struggling.

Then suddenly Federico, who had understood the problem, was at her side.

"Right, young man," he said cheerfully. "Would you like a ride?"

Before Alfredo could reply, he had hoisted him up onto his shoulders and they began the climb together. Sam followed gratefully.

They reached the top and Federico deposited Alfredo carefully on the ground. "Ok?" He said. "High five?"

Alfredo 'High fived' him with glee. "Thank you," he said.

Then he continued "Aren't you the doctor who saved my Nonno's life?"

"Oh," Federico looked surprised. "I didn't realise he was your grandfather. Well, I'm delighted that he is now fit as a fiddle again. All in a day's work." He added.

"Wow, you really are clever. Do you think I could be a doctor one day?"

"I'm sure you could, but you have to work really, really hard at school."

"I do already," Alfredo replied earnestly… and Sam, who had been listening to the exchange attentively said "Oh yes, from what I've heard he really does."

Alfredo beamed happily at the praise.

By this time, Giulia had arrived at the top of the slope with the other children.

She greeted Federico with many thanks and then prepared to shepherd the children back to the classroom.

Federico showed no sign of departing.

"Sam," he said, "you know you asked me if you could see my father's old house? Is this a good time? We could perhaps prepare some lunch together."

"That would be lovely," Sam flushed with pleasure. "Just let me help Giulia back to the classroom with the children. My morning there is done. You go on and I'll follow. I know where it is."

The children were safely installed in the classroom and she explained to Giulia where she was going.

Giulia smiled "Ah!" She said.

"He's just being friendly," Sam protested weakly. "He promised to show me his father's house."

But of course, Giulia didn't believe a word she said.

So she skipped eagerly down the steps to where the small house was situated in a tiny courtyard almost at the bottom of the valley. She realised, looking at the house, that his father really had come from humble beginnings and, by all accounts, had subsequently made a lot of money down in Naples or maybe had married money.

Federico opened the door for her and she followed him into the kitchen. To be more accurate, the whole of the ground floor, apart from a primitive bathroom, was a kitchen come living room with a wooden table and chairs, a battered sofa with a couple of equally battered armchairs and the usual dresser holding mismatched china.

It really was very basic and totally unlike the bustling kitchen at Giulia's house. He saw her gazing around at the bare stone walls with only a couple of framed photos and the inevitable crucifix to ornament them.

"I haven't done anything to improve it for years," he apologised. "I only come here occasionally. It's my, how you say, bolt hole, when I want to get away from the stress of hospital life."

"Please, please don't apologise." Sam said. "I like the simple life. I'm not a great one for material possessions myself."

A steep set of stairs led to two upstairs rooms, one of which had a balcony. He opened the shutters and they walked out. She could see the view of the river and the spot where he had sat beside her the day after the fiasco with the watermelon and the confrontation in the square. She couldn't believe that it was only a few months ago that she had met him and that that meeting had completely changed her life.

I must be sensible, she thought. *I must remember that he is only being friendly because I am Giulia's cousin. I must remember that he has a girlfriend. I must.*

That last she really did not want to remember.

"I wanted to ask you," she said. "I know it's impossible for you to diagnose without examining him, but do you think that anything can be done about Alfredo's condition?"

He considered for a long moment, then he replied. "I can't be sure, as you say, without knowing exactly what is wrong, but I suspect he has a displaced hip which can certainly be corrected when he has finished growing."

"I do hope so," she said quietly, "he is such a lovely little boy and so brave. It was kind of you to come and help today."

He was standing very close to her on the balcony and they were almost touching.

Then they turned at the same moment to go back in. In front of them was the old iron bedstead which belonged to his grandparents and now to him, with its cover hand crocheted, possibly by his grandmother or great grandmother. The bed lay before them, invitingly.

Her heart was beating fast, The tension was palpable.

It was Sam who spoke first, trying to sound light-hearted. "Well, where is that lunch you promised me?"

"Yes, yes of course," he said hastily, gathering his thoughts together. She could only wonder if he had had the same vivid image as herself.

They went down the narrow stairs.

"It won't be a feast," he warned when they were safely down in the kitchen again "far from it. I don't keep much here."

"I'm not expecting one," she smiled. "Give me something to do."

"How about the onion?"

"Ah, the hardest job. Ok," she said.

She reached for the old wooden chopping board behind the sink and found a rather blunt knife.

She peeled and chopped the onion while he opened a tin of tomatoes and put a pot of water on the stove for the pasta. He rooted in the cupboard for tomato paste and a few dried herbs and brought out a packet of dried pasta.

"No cheese," he apologised. "I wasn't expecting visitors." "Oh," he continued, looking at her in concern, "you're crying."

"No, I'm not," she said. "It's the onion."

73

"Of course," he replied. He reached over and wiped the tears from her cheeks. His hand lingered over her face and his eyes, those amazing blue eyes, met hers.

"You are very beautiful," he said, gazing at her, "beautiful and kind."

"Thank you," she said, "and I'm sure my beauty is enhanced by my red streaming eyes from the onion."

"Sorry." He grinned.

He tipped the onion into a saucepan with some oil and they stood together watching as it slowly softened before he poured in the tin of tomatoes, then a dab of tomato paste, some herbs and seasoning.

"It should really simmer for ages," he said, "but let's give it ten minutes shall we, before I put on the pasta?"

"Quite," she said. "I'm not exactly used to Michelin-starred food though your aunt is an amazing cook and Gianfranco is pretty good as well."

He asked her about life with the uncles and she told him how much she enjoyed working in the art gallery with them. She told him about Richard's love of food and Gianfranco's terrible voice, but also how much she adored them both and how lucky she was to be in Italy and have that opportunity.

"And you said you wanted to paint yourself?" He asked.

"Oh, I do a little when I have time," she said offhandedly.

He scrutinised her face "I have a feeling you might be really rather good and you are being modest."

She didn't reply.

"Come, come," he said and he beckoned her over. They sat close together on the battered old sofa that smelt faintly of mould because the house had been unheated for so long.

"Do you remember your grandparents?" She asked.

"Only very vaguely," he said. "It was sad because our life was down in Naples and this village seemed a million miles away when I was young. They never came to visit us and because my father was very busy he rarely had time to bring me here and then my mother wasn't good at keeping in touch after my father died. I feel sorry because I'm sure they would have been glad to see me sometimes, as their grandchild. They both died within a short time of each other and I didn't even attend the funerals because my mother discouraged me, something I regret."

He showed her the old-fashioned photo of the pair of them on their wedding day, staring sternly into the camera lens and then he handed her a photo of his father, taken at the very same school down the hill where she had been that morning and where he was dressed in a smock with a pussycat bow. Some traditions, it seemed, never changed.

She could see why Federico found solace here. She had no idea what life had been like with his mother and stepfather down in Naples, but she understood that this house was the only really tangible link with the father he had lost and who was probably rarely mentioned now. Here he could sit and imagine his father growing up into the young man of almost eighteen before he went to university and qualified as a doctor.

She smoothed the photo with her hand and smiled at it. "He looks kind," she said.

"He was. And fun," he added wistfully, "he made us laugh, both my mother and I. My mother doesn't laugh much these days."

They gazed together at the youthful face looking up at them from the photo.

Finally, he took it from her and replaced it on the shelf. He took a deep breath as if gathering his thoughts together.

"Time, I think, for our gourmet meal."

"Can't wait," she grinned.

When the water was boiling, he put the pasta in and they waited a while. Finally, he removed a strand and held it up for her to test, dangling it in front of her mouth. "Al dente?" He asked.

"Yes, definitely to the tooth," she laughed.

He drained it and mixed it in the sauce. Then they sat at the rickety table and ate. He removed a speck of tomato from her cheek and his hand lingered again on her face. There was a spoonful of sauce left in the pan and she fed it to him, laughing.

"Next time," said, "I will take you out for a proper meal."

"I would like that," she said, thrilled at the thought there would be a next time. She was tempted to say "What about about Nadia?" But kept silent, unwilling to break the spell.

When they had finished she washed the two pans.

Finally, he said. "Sorry, sorry, I must go. I'm on duty again in a few hours."

He locked the house while she waited then they walked together to the point where she had to return to Giulia's house.

He leant forward and after a moment's hesitation kissed her on both cheeks, lingering near her mouth with the second one but, despite her yearning for a proper kiss, it never came.

She watched him go towards his car at the bottom of the hill. At the last moment, he turned and waved a hand and she returned the wave. Then she waited until he was long out of sight on the road back to Naples.

As meals go, she thought, that was probably one of the best I've ever had And it had nothing, absolutely nothing at all to do with the food.

Chapter 9

Giulia and Sam were both dressed in their best outfits.

It was an important day for them and for the village as there was going to be a christening, always a source of joy as a new inhabitant joined the population, signifying hope and growth for the future. They walked together to Alfredo's house on the eastern side of the village, climbing up and down steps and through a dozen different little flower-filled courtyards, their high heels click-clacking on the stone, nodding and smiling to everyone they passed. Everyone knew where they were going and there were many cries of "Auguri," 'best wishes'.

The house, sporting a large blue rosette on the front door to denote the birth of a baby boy, was already a hive of activity when they arrived, with friends and relations gathering, food being prepared and of course, the baby being dressed in his lace christening robe.

"That used to be mine," said Alfredo proudly, because of course, it was his new baby brother who was being baptised. He himself was wearing a smart new waistcoat and tie bought especially for the occasion, with his hair slicked back.

Sam had been both thrilled and surprised to be invited. Giulia was to be a godmother because she was Alfredo's teacher, but he had asked his parents to invite Sam as well and they had gladly agreed as they had heard how kind she had been to him. Sam was especially pleased to be there as she knew Federico had been asked to be a godfather. He would be an honoured guest because he had saved the life of Alfredo's grandfather Paolo and Paolo's son and daughter-in-law owed him a huge debt of gratitude. He was already there and smiled at Sam as she entered the house, making her heart miss a beat once again.

Eventually, everyone assembled and the whole group walked in procession, as was the custom, up to the church, passing even more assembled villagers applauding on the way and wishing them 'Auguri', best wishes. The baby, carried by his father, was of course the centre of attention, but oblivious to the congratulations being showered on the family as he was fast asleep. Alfredo held Sam's hand as he manfully coped with the hundreds of steps and she, once again, was amazed at his fortitude and courage.

It was a Sunday and they sat in the front pews during the mass with Sam trying to follow the service. She was acutely aware of Federico sitting in front of her with Giulia as godparents and she wondered if he was aware of her studying the back of his head.

The mass over, the congregation, or most of them, stayed on to watch the christening. The parents and godparents moved to the font and the baby was handed to Federico as the godfather. He in turn brought the baby forward and handed him to the priest who, after dipping his hand in the holy water, blessed the child and made the sign of the cross on his forehead. The baby had woken by this time and gazed wide-eyed up at the priest, but didn't make a sound. Alfredo as the big brother was standing importantly by the font.

The baby was named Paolo after his grandfather as was the tradition, but he was also given the name Federico.

Sam, glancing at Federico's face when this was announced, saw him flush with pleasure. He obviously hadn't realised that this was going to happen. Sam was so happy for him, that the baby was going to bear his name. The godparents made their vows, to look after the child and be responsible for his welfare, then he was handed back to Federico to hold.

Sam saw the look of tenderness on his face as he looked down at his namesake and thought what a wonderful father he was going to be one day. Then, as she gazed at him, he turned and looked at her. She nodded approvingly and he smiled back.

Then they all left the church and proceeded down the hill to the house, passing groups of villagers once again congratulating the family.

At the party afterwards, Alfredo was the star of the show, proudly showing off his new brother who was passed from relative to relative around the room without complaining at each new set of arms and faces exclaiming how handsome he was and how like his grandfather. Gifts were given, mostly silver and gold jewellery, little medallions bearing the image of Saint Paul. By coincidence, he had been born on the 29th of June, the Saints Day and the same birthday as his grandfather Paolo. Photos were taken of the family and the godparents and especially with old Paulo, now fully fit and well, sitting proudly with his two grandsons in the chair of honour. They all toasted the baby with Prosecco and the usual bonbonierre were handed out, the little lace parcels of sugared almonds with a small slip of paper inside bearing the baby's name.

Sam had racked her brains for a suitable present to give him, but eventually decided on a frame into which she intended to put a painting of Alfredo and his brother.

Federico came over to talk to her.

"Well done," she said, "you have a namesake. You must be very proud."

"It was as much a surprise to me as to everyone else," he confessed. "I had no idea they were going to call him Federico."

"You deserve it," she said, "they are very grateful to you. He might not have had a grandfather if you hadn't been there."

"I was only doing my job," he said modestly. "Anyway," he looked at her with an amused expression, "it's a day that I shall always remember for other reasons. It's not often I get someone yelling at me, in front of a crowd of people too, telling me that I am rude and arrogant. It took me a while to process that fact."

Sam blushed. "Don't remind me. I still shudder when I think of it, but I do have to say in my defence that I was pretty shocked to be shoved like that. It might not have been just the melon that came to grief."

They both laughed, then he said more seriously. "I enjoyed our lunch together in my father's house." He paused then continued. "I was wondering if one day we could…" but he got no further as at that moment Alfredo came bouncing up to ask what she thought of the picture he had drawn and the moment was lost.

She could have cried with frustration. Was he going to ask her to his father's house again, or for a meal? She would never know. She turned her attention, with difficulty, to Alfredo's picture and the moment had gone.

Federico made no further attempt to speak to her, apart from saying goodbye, almost as if he regretted what he had been about to say. He made his excuses and left, explaining that he had to return to work. As he left the room, he turned and his gaze lingered over her. He smiled ruefully. Whatever words he had been about to utter were lost and she could only torment herself by wondering.

Chapter 10

It was the day of the school outing and an excited crocodile of children filed down the hill to the waiting coach. She herself was excited too as the uncles had long promised her a visit to Caserta, the palace of the king of the Kingdom of the two Sicilies, but there had never been enough time to take her.

They passed smiling villagers wishing them a buona giornata, a good day and one of the little girls called out "We're going to see the king!"

"Not exactly," she explained to a puzzled group of villagers. "We're going to Caserta and though Giulia has explained several times that there hasn't been a king there for many, many years, some of them don't want to believe it. They're going to be very disappointed I'm afraid. Not only no king, but no one even wearing a crown."

They piled onto the bus and there was a scuffle between small groups of children as to who was to sit next to Sam on one of the two front seats. Sam was secretly delighted when Alfredo won the tussle.

It was nearly an hour and a half's journey and Sam and Giulia had debated long and hard as to whether it was a good idea to go such a long way with young children, but in the end, they had decided it was worth the effort. Some of the children had never even been outside the village or even in a coach and they gazed out of the windows in astonishment when the coach left the twisting mountain roads and joined the autostrada with its roaring traffic and enormous lorries, passing through several towns.

Giulia kept up a constant flow of singing to pass the time and also to keep the children in their seats as some of the more obstreperous boys wanted to try and race up and down the aisle, so it took all of Giulia's sternest warnings to keep them in their places.

A few of the children had already opened their lunch boxes and both Sam and Giulia had to try and deter them from eating everything or there would have been problems later on when they stopped for their picnic and the greedy ones would have had nothing to eat.

Alfredo proudly showed Sam his new red backpack. "It's a present from Dr Federico. He's not really my godfather, only my brother's, but he said that because I am so good at looking after him I deserved a present too."

"I am sure you do deserve it." Sam smiled, thinking that that was just typical of Federico to be so thoughtful.

They arrived at last and Giulia marshalled the excited children into a crocodile again as they left the coach and went through the entrance gates. They had all been given new orange caps so they could be seen easily as there were several other school parties and Giulia's greatest dread was losing one of the children.

"Wow," they said as they saw the enormous palace that lay before them.

"Now," Giulia said, "who can tell me the person who lived here?"

"The King," they all chorused.

Then one child asked. "But why isn't there a king here anymore?"

"That's because a long time ago this part of our country was like a separate state, a different country if you like. It was called the Kingdom of the two Sicilies and it was joined up with the island of Sicily. Then, because there were lots of little states all with different people in charge, they decided to all join together and we became one big country called Italy."

"And this king who lived here was the king of Italy?"

"No, that was much later on and he was a different king. He was called Victor Emmanuel and he lived far away up in the north in a city called Turin."

"Why? Why?"

Ah, the eternal Why? thought Sam.

"So, why haven't we got a king now?" A puzzled child asked.

"That's because people in Italy decided a long time ago that they didn't want a king any more."

"Why?"

"Because," Giulia glanced at Sam and raised her eyebrows, "because they wanted to be what is called a republic and have a president decided by the people."

"Oh, that's a shame."

"Anyway," Giulia said, trying to get the conversation back on track, "this palace is the biggest royal palace in the world and it did have a king in it. Can anyone tell me his name?"

"Carlo, Charles like the English king," Alfredo chimed in.

"Well done, Alfredo…and after him?"

"Ferdinand," someone else shouted.

"Excellent," Giulia said. Then, feeling they had discussed the king long enough, she said, "Can anyone guess how many rooms the palace has?"

"300?"

"A lot, lot more."

"A million!"

"No, not as many as that."

"One thousand."

"Much better. It's one thousand and two hundred."

"Wow, wow, that's an awful lot. Did the king live in all of them?"

"I don't think so," Giulia laughed. "He had what is called the Royal Apartments and we will go and see them, but he had many, many people working for him, people looking after the country, lots of soldiers, people working in the library and the museum so they all had to have somewhere to live. And," she added, "Guess how many windows there are?"

After a few more wild guesses the number was revealed to be one thousand, seven hundred and forty-three. The children were wide-eyed with amazement. One little boy said "My house only has," …he counted on his fingers, "Six!"

They entered the palace and Giulia whispered to Sam, "I never realised explaining Italian history could be so difficult." Sam grinned.

The children looked in awe at all the glittering gold, the huge wide staircase, the marble floors, the enormous chandeliers and the pictures and statues everywhere. They fell silent, never having seen anything like it before. One little girl, almost frightened at the enormity of it all, looked almost on the verge of tears. "It's too big," she whispered. "You could get lost here."

Sam reached for her hand. "You won't get lost," she reassured her. "Just hold my hand and we'll go round together."

They went into the bedroom where the bed was draped in curtains.

"It's like a tent," they said. "Why did the king sleep in a tent?"

"I expect it kept him warm," Sam said.

"I'm hungry," wailed one little boy.

"Right," Giulia said, seeing that some of the children were flagging. "That's enough, time for lunch."

There was a cheer. They went out into the grounds and found a picnic spot where they ate their lunch. Sam noted that Alfredo was very careful with Federico's rucksack.

When they had finished and rested for a while Giulia lead them through the English Garden, or at least part of it because it was so big.

"Is this what your garden in England is like?" One of the children asked Sam.

Sam laughed. "No, I think this one was made for the king. People in England usually only have very little gardens."

They were even more overawed by the huge canal stretching away into the distance and the enormous fountains with statues in them. Some of the boys wanted to go into the water, but Giulia firmly vetoed it.

All too soon, it was time to climb back into the coach, take the autostrada and wend their way back up the mountain road to the village where the parents were there to meet them.

The children ran off chattering excitedly to their mothers and fathers, telling them everything they had seen that day.

"It was enormous," said one child, stretching his arms as wide as they could go.

"But we didn't see the king though," said another earnestly.

"Ah well," Giulia smiled at Sam, "I hope they at least learnt something today even if it was only that not all the English have gardens as big as Caserta. Thank you so much Sam for helping me today."

Sam smiled, "I enjoyed the trip. I love to be with the children," but her eyes were on the little departing figure of Alfredo holding his father's hand, telling him all about the day and particularly she was looking at the little red rucksack that Federico had given him, bobbing up and down as he hobbled along.

Chapter 11

Sam was particularly excited because it was going to be a very special weekend. She was on her way to the village again and it was the night of Ferragosto. The 15th of August was a landmark celebration in Italy which originated, Giulia had told her, from the festival of the Emperor Augustus, a day of rest after all the hard work on the farms and businesses.

It was the beginning of the holiday season in Italy when all workers were given leave. The gallery was closed for a week too so the uncles were coming as well, with the promise of drinking and dancing ("and eating!." Uncle Richard added hopefully) and even, Giulia promised, fireworks at the end of the evening.

Most of the shops and all the factories in Naples were closed during this period and they were all glad to get out of the city. It had been a particularly hot summer and most people in Italy flocked to the seaside or the mountains when they could. It had been difficult to sleep in the sweltering heat and they were all looking forward to the cooler air of the village.

As they drove to the foot of the hill and parked, they could see the bright bunting adorning the square above them. They walked up with Richard puffing and panting and Gianfranco nagging him that he really must lose some weight and Richard telling him to stop nagging for once and just let him enjoy the evening, and then he would start dieting tomorrow.

"Fat chance," Gianfranco muttered.

A platform had been laid out in the square for a show and, later on, dancing. They were warmly welcomed at Giulia's house and after the usual sumptuous spread made by the indefatigable Maria and a final glass (or two in Richard's case) of the delicious liqueur made out of tiny wild strawberries, a speciality of the village, the whole group moved to the square.

Enrico, in his official capacity as mayor, had arranged a festival. Chairs had been put out for the older people and Maria, after all her hard work, sank gratefully into one of them followed by the uncles on either side of her.

"Phew," said Richard, fanning himself with his hanky, "Good to get a little breeze."

Sam found herself looking anxiously around.

"What is it?" Giulia whispered.

"Oh, nothing," Sam replied. "I was just looking at the people in the windows and on the balconies. They have ringside seats for everything."

Secretly, of course, she was looking out for Federico, but there was no sign of him. Maybe he was working or, worse still, at the seaside with Nadia. A fierce pang of jealousy shot through her.

The square was also packed with visitors, not just villagers, all escaping the heat of the city.

A troupe of dancers arrived in traditional costume, a soft white bodice and black velvet skirt with a red sash for the women, and red shirts, black waistcoat for the men. And the dancing began.

"It's the tarantella," Giulia explained. "It's associated with the bite of the tarantula. Apparently if you danced in a frenzied manner you could cure the spider's bite. Now it is more a dance for lovers."

A little group of musicians took their place at the side of the stage, an accordion player, a tambourine, a mandolin and a guitar. They began to play and the dance began, the dancers whirling frantically, their feet seemingly hardly touching the ground.

Sam, absorbed in the dancing, hadn't noticed a figure appear beside her. The dance finished and they all applauded and there were cries of "Bravo, bravissimo!"

"Ciao Sam."

She whirled around, startled to see Federico standing behind her.

"Oh hello, how are you?" She stammered.

"Fine," he said. "Good to see you and good to get away from the heat." He drew up a chair beside her. "Did you enjoy the dance?"

"Yes, very much. I hear it started from a spider bite."

"Yes, so they say. It's also linked to St Vitus, a frantic dancing caused by an illness."

"Well, you are the doctor, you should know," laughed Giulia, joining them. He greeted her by kissing her on both cheeks. "You should have come earlier for supper," she added.

"I didn't finish at the hospital until late and came straight up. Thanks all the same. Everyone else is at the seaside so I thought I'd come and join the fun."

By 'everyone' thought Sam, he meant Nadia. Still he had taken the trouble to drive up after a long day so that must mean something.

The dancers had left the stage and in their place came a solitary figure in a stark black suit. The musicians struck up and the singer began 'O Sole Mio'. Sam couldn't help but glance at Gianfranco sitting a short distance away, fervently hoping he wouldn't join in.

The song dedicated to the sun of Naples finished with thunderous applause. 'Santa Lucia' was next and was greeted by loud cheers. It was followed by 'Torna a Sorrento', return to Sorrento, and finally 'Volare'. Sam found herself clapping as wildly as the rest and there were quite a few of the elderly villagers wiping tears from their eyes, listening to all the old traditional Neapolitan songs.

Sadly the concert was over at last, but the musicians played on. Giulia's father rose to his feet and bowed to his wife, offering a hand in invitation. She graciously accepted and they took to the dance floor to loud cheers and applause from the assembled company. They moved together in a practised way and Sam couldn't help but be touched by the sight of them obviously still enamoured of each other despite many years together and they were also surprisingly nimble.

"Don't be surprised," Giulia said, seeing Sam watching them. "My mother was very sought after apparently when she was young and I was told she lead my father a merry dance before she finally accepted him."

"I can well believe it," laughed Sam.

Giulia was claimed by one of the visitors and soon the floor was packed. She waited awkwardly, acutely aware of him next to her.

"Well," said Federico at last, "we may as well, how do you say in English? Give it a whirl."

"I'm not sure I know the steps," she said.

"I'll teach you," he smiled at her and her heart lurched. She hoped he couldn't feel her trembling as he took her hand and led her onto the floor.

After a few false starts, she soon got the hang of it and they were soon twirling with the rest, laughing as they whirled and twisted around.

The next dance was a communal one where they all joined hands and danced in a circle, moving backwards and forwards. She was afraid he would then go off and dance with someone else, but he showed no sign of abandoning her. He seemed eager to teach her every new step. The dance got more and more frantic and finished with an energetic spin where she nearly overbalanced and found herself falling.

He caught her and held her tightly. For a moment their eyes met and she couldn't breathe. Then he seemed to collect himself and he looked away abruptly.

But still he didn't leave her side and the tempo of the music changed to a slow dance. He put his arm around her waist and they moved together as one. She closed her eyes and felt his breath on her cheek as they swayed to the soft romantic music. She was acutely aware of his body against hers.

"If this is heaven," she thought dreamily, "then I am there." She couldn't imagine a more romantic evening than this, a starlit night with music playing, in what was turning out to be her favourite place in entire world, dancing with someone she was falling deeply in love with.

Then as the music slowed and finally came to an end she opened her eyes to find him staring at her with the most extraordinary expression, almost of shock.

"I'm sorry, so sorry," he said, "please, forgive me. I must go."

And go he did, abruptly turning away and plunging down the steps as if he couldn't wait to escape.

She stood, shattered, gazing after him as he disappeared from view, wanting to cry out in pain.

She was shocked to the core and a moment later shocked again by a huge explosion.

She twisted around frantically and then realised it was the first of the fireworks exploding on the hill opposite the village.

She was dimly aware of Giulia beside her, "Here we go," Giulia shouted in glee.

Each explosion was like a dagger in her heart. While the crowd cheered and whistled and 'oohed' and 'aahed' every time a fresh cascade of stars rained from the heavens she felt numb. The evening had held so much promise. There was no doubt he felt something for her, but then to leave so abruptly: she couldn't bear it.

The fireworks ended at last and then a cry went up "Fuoco, fire!"

Despite her feelings of despair, she realised that the hillside opposite was ablaze. It was predictable really with the conditions so dry. Men could be seen running frantically around trying to quell the flames with buckets of water.

Giulia's brothers were enchanted. "Best bit of the evening," they chorused. They were quite disappointed when the flames were extinguished at last.

They all returned to the house for a nightcap, then Richard and Gianfranco went down to the hotel at the bottom of the hill and Sam, after helping to clear up, took to her bed, grateful for the darkness and privacy to shed the tears she had managed so far to hold back. It was impossible, this roller coaster of emotion. One moment they seemed so close, the next, he was so distant.

What on earth was happening?

Chapter 12

The uncles took her to Matera. "Of all the places in Italy you must visit," Gianfranco told her, "this is the most unusual."

They drove through the countryside for three hours, almost to the other coast, with the uncles changing places in the driving seat every so often, not to mention frequent stops to refuel on strong espresso and, for Richard, a cake or two, much to Gianfranco's disapproval. In Richard's case the mantra 'eat to live' was very much reversed to 'live to eat' and it was no use Gianfranco repeatedly saying, "Ricardo caro, you must not eat so much. You will be ill."

The countryside through which they drove was rugged and bare.

"It's not called the Mezzogiorno, midday, for nothing," Richard told her. "The sun is so strong and the soil so dry and rocky it's hard to farm here. That's why it has always been poorer down in the south. Goats are the only animals to do well because they eat anything."

They arrived in Matera at last and Sam gasped at the view before her. They hadn't been exaggerating. It was more than unusual. A whole city lay before here, plunging down into a valley. On the lower level were layer upon layer of caves with a more modern city built above with large buildings and wide streets.

"They call it 'The Sassi', the Stones," Richard said. "It's the third oldest troglodyte city in the world after Aleppo and Jericho. They reckon people have lived in caves here for more than 7, 000 years."

"Yes, but it was a hard life with many of them becoming ill with diseases like malaria," Gianfranco added. "They didn't have sanitation or running water. They only moved out in the 1950s."

"And that was only after a public outcry," Richard was vying to continue the story. "It was called 'The Shame of Italy' but it has to be said that many of the citizens didn't want to go because, despite the awful conditions, it was a close community. I suppose a little like the back-to-back houses in England in pre-war years without proper sanitation. They were friendly places where everyone helped each other."

"Yes, I know what you mean," Sam said. "Then in England, they were moved into soulless tower blocks where people felt isolated and lonely. I suppose the people here were put into those modern blocks of flats that we can see higher up."

"Exactly...and the caves left to the wolves." Gianfranco added. "Though there aren't any wolves here now," he said hastily.

They wandered through the small alleyways and often, as Gianfranco pointed out, across the top of other caves. "It was made a UNESCO World Heritage site in 1993 and European capital of culture in 2019. Some of the caves are now fancy hotels, but they have preserved the rock churches and there's a cave museum created by Byzantine monks with wonderful frescoed interiors. We can show you that after lunch if you like," Richard said brightly, thinking of food again, though it was never very far from his thoughts.

They had a long lunch in one of the many cave restaurants that had sprung up since Matera had become a tourist destination. Gianfranco watched disapprovingly as Richard had second helpings.

"You can never have too much of a good thing," Richard replied, though he did look a little ill from overindulgence on the wine. Sam hoped Gianfranco would insist on driving on the way back.

Then the uncles said, "You go and explore some more while we have a little nap in the shade, ready for the return journey."

So Sam left them and wandered off through the little alleyways again. She found one with a recreation of what it must have been like to live in the caves, bare rock without light, a few sticks of furniture and a cooking pot over what would have been an open fire. It must have been so cold and comfortless in winter.

Emerging into the light she heard voices behind her. One of them was familiar.

She whirled around.

Federico was standing not ten yards away on the pathway amongst a group of men and women in suits.

He saw her staring and then she could see him mutter something to the group and he came across to her.

"What are you doing here?" He kissed her politely on both cheeks.

She explained about the uncles. "And you?"

"Oh a medical conference. It's our afternoon break." He hesitated. "Have you seen everything?"

"Not yet. It's so huge. I want to see one of the rock churches."

"I will take you to my favourite place. Just a moment."

He retreated and said a few words to the assembled group. They gazed at her and she smiled back. One of them gave an appreciative nod and a knowing look and she could see what some of the men were thinking.

"Come," he said. He took her hand and led her along the alleyway.

He seemed uncomfortable and she wondered if he was remembering about the way he had left during the dancing up at the village. She decided that she would say nothing, just enjoy being with him.

They walked in silence and after about ten minutes they arrived.

"This is the Convent of the Santa Lucia alle Malve, the Convent of the Mallows," he explained. "It's the first female convent of the Benedictines. It is one of the oldest and the frescoes are twelfth, maybe even eleventh century. Wonderful, aren't they?"

He was still holding her hand and they gazed together at the frescoes. "They are in such an amazing condition considering they are so old."

"I suppose because there was so little light it would have helped preserve them, and they would have just have had candles," she said.

She was acutely conscious of his arm brushing hers.

"Exactly."

Then, abruptly, he swung her around. The kiss when it came was as long and thrilling as it was unexpected. Her body melted into his.

He released her at last and everything she was feeling for him was in her eyes as she gazed at him.

"Damn you," he said violently and she was taken aback at the ferocity of his words. "I have tried so hard to resist you and I think about you all the time. All the time. But I cannot get involved with you, I cannot," he added despairingly.

"Involved!" She burst out, irrationally furious. "I'm sorry if I am an inconvenience, an impediment to your plans." She was beyond embarrassment at the tears flowing more freely now.

He was taken aback, a look of shock on his face at her words.

"Oh you stupid, stupid man, you stupid, stupid man," she shouted, her words echoing around the cave. "Stupid," as if emphasising everything she said. She turned and fled out of the cave and back up the alleyway.

"Wait," he called after her urgently. "You will get lost. Please wait. You don't understand. Please let me explain."

But she plunged on heedlessly, round rock after rock, not knowing where she was going, but just desperate to get as far away as possible from him. Finally she reached a path leading upwards to the piazza above the Sassi and found the place where the uncles were waiting.

"Are you alright?" They chorused, looking anxiously at her distraught face.

"Yes, I'm fine," she said, "trying to collect herself. It's just that I got lost and panicked." She took a long drink of water and wiped her face, scraping her hair back in a ponytail so she felt cooler.

They found the car and she curled up on the back seat. Despite it all, she could still feel the pressure of his lips on hers, the hunger. There was strong emotion there, not a mere flirtation, she could sense that. If he really cared, what was it that was holding him back?

Nadia of course.

The uncles knew something had upset her, but they were far too tactful to say so. There was a silence in the car save for the occasional tuneless singing by Gianfranco which made her smile despite herself and brought her some measure of comfort.

Chapter 13

The gallery was busy, but Richard, ever hungry, had asked Sam to go out and buy pastries from the local bar, together with three coffees.

She was on her way along the crowded street when she nearly bumped into the tall, elegant woman walking towards her.

"Mi scusi, sorry," she muttered and then stopped abruptly.

It was Nadia.

Nadia looked at her quizzically for a moment, then obviously recognised her.

"Sam?" She said. "Sam from the art gallery? I think you are a friend of Federico's cousin Giulia?"

"Yes, that's right," Sam stood awkwardly not knowing how to continue the conversation. Nadia was so elegant and as Sam's eyes appraised her she knew that Nadia's whole outfit must have cost the same as Sam's yearly salary. Her blonde hair was long and sleek, made so by an expensive hair stylist and her smooth olive skin wore minimum makeup yet she still managed to look like a super model.

"Do you have time for a quick coffee?" Nadia asked.

Sam demurred, thinking that the uncles would be missing her, but then decided that a quick coffee wouldn't hurt. They didn't even need to sit down as Italians in general just paid for their espresso and stood at the counter, drank quickly and left. It was usually only the tourists who sat and lingered over their cappuccinos in the sunshine.

"I love art. It must be so nice working in a gallery. I wish I could draw and paint." Nadia said smiling. At least her lips were smiling, but maybe Sam imagined it, there was a wary expression in her eyes which were giving out a different message to that which her lips were saying.

"Thank you," Sam said. Then she realised she must return the compliment. "I could never do what you do. Federico tells me you are a lawyer."

"Yes, I am, " Nadia didn't expand.

There was an awkward pause and then she said casually. "Have you seen much of Federico? He seems to go to the village much more these days than he used to?"

"Well," Sam said, trying to sound equally casual. "I've bumped into him a few times. Oh and of course, he came to Pompeii with Giulia and me as he said he hadn't been there for a while. I think he likes to come to the village because it reminds him of his father and his roots. I understand he was brought up near your family in Naples."

She was trying hard to bring the conversation round again. She omitted to mention the meeting in Matera in case he hadn't told her. At least not the full story, obviously.

"Yes, that's right. We have known each other since we were babies. I suppose you're right that he wants to explore his roots," she said dubiously, but she didn't sound convinced.

Is she jealous? thought Sam. Then that would suppose she feels she has reason to be jealous which means she is not sure of Federico's feelings for her.

103

Nadia continued to probe gently. "Are you staying in Italy long? I mean, is this a temporary job with your uncle and are you planning to move on?" There was a note of optimism in her voice, but Sam had to disappoint her by saying "No, no, I want to stay as long as my uncle needs me. I really like working in the gallery and I want to keep developing my art as well. I love this country…and the people."

Nadia didn't say, "and one person in particular," but Sam sensed that was on her mind.

Sam couldn't help herself. She asked curiously, "Do you remember Federico's father?"

There was another pause.

"A little. He died when we were both nine. He and my father were best friends and I remember my mother and father crying with his mother. It was a difficult time in everyone's life."

"But they like his stepfather, your parents I mean?"

"Oh yes, he is another friend from our circle." She made it sound as if it was an exclusive club. "He had lost his own wife so it is nice that they got together, both of them lonely."

It was a sweet thing to say and Sam thought that if the situation was not as it was she might actually like Nadia.

"Yes, that is good," Sam said. Then she added. "I must go. I'm supposed to be at work and my uncle is expecting me. Let me pay for the coffee."

"No, no, already done," said Nadia.

"Well, that's very kind. Thank you," Sam said.

She turned to go, then suddenly remembered what she was supposed to have come for. "Oh, how silly, Uncle Richard's cakes! He'll kill me if I don't get them. Goodbye, nice to have met you again."

Nadia walked off and Sam gazed after her, thrown by the encounter and wondering at the undertones of their meeting and what exactly had been implied by Nadia's questions.

She was woken from her reverie by the insistent voice of the barista enquiring what it was that she would like to order.

She paid and carried the cakes and coffee back to the gallery where Richard and Gianfranco were wondering why she had been so long.

She explained that she had met a friend and had been delayed and Richard fell ravenously on his cake like a starving man who had been lost in the jungle for three weeks, disappointed that she hadn't brought an extra.

"You can have mine," Sam said, offering it to him. "I'm not really hungry."

"Are you sure?" Richard said, but it was already halfway to his mouth.

Sam spent the rest of the day wondering about the encounter with Nadia and had to fight hard to concentrate on the job in hand. Towards evening when they at last closed up she was able to go to her room and be alone with her thoughts.

***

It wasn't only Nadia who noticed that Federico was coming to the village much more often these days. Giulia had remarked on it, especially when it always seemed to coincide with Sam's visits. Once, in fact, he had come when Sam wasn't there and although he tried to conceal his disappointment, she could see he was taken aback. She had looked quizzically at her friend, but Sam had given her the same reason she had given to Nadia. It was just a coincidence and perhaps he was feeling the need to go back to his roots. Giulia though wasn't convinced, but she wisely kept her thoughts to herself.

She was only worried that he would break Sam's heart and that was the last thing she wanted for someone who was fast becoming a treasured friend.

Chapter 14

Over the next few months, several of the young men who wandered into the gallery asked her out, but she fancied none of them.

One though, persisted. His name was Alberto and he was an architect, a pleasant enough young man who was always polite and kind and the uncles liked him so, after several refusals, she agreed to be taken out to dinner. Then he took her on a boat trip around the bay of Naples where they saw dolphins frolicking in the waves; then another day a drive around the hairpin bends of the rugged Amalfi coast with the little towns of Sorrento and Positano clinging to the cliffs. There were lemon groves and pastel-hued houses leading down to a spectacular azure sea. It was breath taking. They swam in the sea from a secluded beach, then had lunch at a little trattoria and Sam could see where the expression 'La dolce Vita' 'the sweet life' came from.

They visited elegant Ravello where Alberto told her world-famous music festivals were held. They entered cool churches and busy markets; they joined in the passeggiata, the evening walk among the town's people, and watched the sunset together, waiting for that final green flash as it finally disappeared below the horizon. Then he kissed her.

It had been a perfect day. Almost. She could have persuaded herself that she was really attracted to him, but always there was that spectre of Federico haunting her. When she closed her eyes for the kiss, she could see Federico's face, not Alberto's and could imagine the touch of his lips on hers.

Then one day, they were strolling hand in hand along the Lungomare, the seafront in Naples. They had eaten their supper in the pretty little fishing village of Borgo Marinari looking out at the many sailboats bobbing on the waves, jostling for space. Alberto, always with a fund of stories, told her the sad tale of the siren Partenope who was rejected by the wandering Ulysses and was reputed to be buried somewhere on that spot.

They were wandering past the park with its duck fountain and the packed hotels and restaurants that lined the seafront. In the distance, they could see both Vesuvius and the Isle of Capri bathed in the orange light of the setting sun.

Above them stood the Castel d'Ovo and music floated down from the terraces. It was all so very romantic, one of the most beautiful walks in the world, Sam thought, and with Alberto by her side, she could almost imagine being in love with him. Looking up at the castle, where lights were beginning to appear she said to Alberto "Doesn't that mean Egg Castle? What a strange name!"

"Yes," he laughed, "the Roman poet Virgil had a reputation as a sorcerer and a predictor of the future. He is supposed to have put a magical egg in the foundation to support it. If the egg was ever broken the castle would have been destroyed and a series of disastrous events would follow for Naples. Luckily it seems never to have been broken which is good news both for the castle and for us." They both laughed.

They stopped to buy an ice cream, as usual Sam dithering about which flavour to choose from the dozens on display. Alberto suggested that they choose their own and then swap halfway to which Sam happily agreed. They tried to do that, but although it was evening, it was still very warm and the ice cream was melting faster than they could eat it.

Alberto produced a clean handkerchief and was busily mopping Sam's chin and dabbing her hand which was covered in delicious pistachio and they were both laughing when Sam looked over his shoulder and suddenly saw Federico walking arm and arm with Nadia, coming slowly towards them. There was no way of avoiding them.

She gave a sharp intake of breath.

"What is it?" Alberto was alarmed.

"Oh nothing." She tried to gather herself. "Just some people I know."

He turned "Ah, Federico," he said.

"You know each other?"

"Not well, but we were at university at the same time and of course he was studying medicine and I architecture, but our paths crossed quite a few times over the years."

He went forward and shook Federico's hand. Sam followed slowly.

"Ciao, Sam." Federico said and Nadia inclined her head with a fixed smile of acknowledgement and Federico introduced Nadia to Alberto They stood for a few minutes making polite conversation, the men more than the two women who were both covertly eyeing each other warily. Nadia must be happy seeing me with Alberto, Sam thought, if she was worried about Federico's feelings for me. Federico was catching up with Alberto's career and vice versa, but Sam had a feeling that Federico was distracted and his gaze kept wandering towards her, but as she returned his gaze, he looked away hastily. If she hadn't known any better, she could almost have thought he was jealous.

"I'm being fanciful," she told herself but as they said their final goodbyes and walked on she took Alberto's hand and leant her head on his shoulder. She felt slightly guilty about using Alberto in this way but if there really any possibility of Federico being jealous, she thought she was going to play up to it for all she was worth.

One thing was certain though, was that any idea she may have had that she was falling in love with Alberto was now firmly out of the window. There was only one person she was in love with and that was Federico.

Chapter 15

When she wasn't up in the village, working in the gallery, out with the uncles, learning Italian or seeing Alberto, Sam sketched and painted, which didn't of course leave much time. By using every scrap of time left to her she had built up quite a portfolio of pictures. Most of what she did of the village was done from memory: the old lady with the donkey bringing the wood that she had encountered on that first, fateful day when she had met Federico: the narrow village streets with their steep steps and flower-filled balconies; cats lying on terracotta tiled roofs, old ladies dressed in black gossiping on corners, the busy square on market day with fruit and vegetables piled high, the old men in their flat caps and flannel shirts playing cards at the cafe and, especially delightful, was the old man peeling and eating a raw onion with a carafe of red wine at his side, a slice of onion and a glug of wine alternately, his red nose testifying to a lifetime of the latter. Then there were the little groups of people meeting during the evening walk in the square with everyone dressed in their best and the black-robed priest standing at the church door to greet his parishioners.

The village was an endless source of inspiration and frustration set in when she didn't have time to get all her ideas down on paper so she found herself getting up at dawn before the uncles were awake and creeping out onto the balcony which was already getting the first rays of the sun creeping over the horizon.

The city woke slowly and when inspiration from the village was scarce she would sketch and paint Neapolitan life emerging into a new day: women hanging washing out on balconies in streets that were often so narrow they could lean over and almost shake hands with each other; children skipping on their way to school; shopkeepers in long aprons sweeping the pavement in front of their shops; the cafes opening up early to serve coffees and pastries to the workers: sometimes there would be whole families riding to work and school on a single Vespa or a little three-wheeled Ape piled high with someone's worldly goods perched precariously on the back.

Then one day, absorbed in her work she was surprised by Uncle Richard opening the door behind her.

"So, this is where you are hiding," he said.

"Buongiorno," she said.

He stretched and yawned.

"Buongiorno Sam. Another lovely day in paradise."

Then he peered over her shoulder. She was painting a little vignette of three women gossiping on the street corner, their heads together as they exchanged some particularly spicy piece of tittle-tattle.

She was acutely conscious of him staring down. "Just a hobby," she started to say, "It amuses me to do it."

"Have you got any others?"

She went to her bedroom to fetch her portfolio. He slowly spread them out on the kitchen table.

"They're not very good," Sam apologised.

He looked up. "Not very good? They are wonderful, Sam. Why have you never shown me these before? You have really captured the essence of southern Italian life. I love them." He turned and shouted to Gianfranco to come and look.

A sleepy Gianfranco appeared at the kitchen door, "Che successo? What's happening? Is there a fire?"

He joined Richard at the table, "Madonna, Sam! Did you do these? They are favoloso, wonderful. We must have an exhibition."

Sam coloured up, "No, no, you don't have to flatter me. They are just a bit of fun," she protested.

"Sam, Sam," said her uncle. "Believe me; these pictures are seriously good. They will sell to the tourists and the locals like hot cakes."

"Hot cakes?" Gianfranco's English was good, but he looked puzzled. "What have cakes got to do with these pictures?"

They laughed and Richard translated, but Gianfranco was still puzzled.

And so it was that Richard, Gianfranco and Sam set to work carefully mounting and framing Sam's pictures. It took a few weeks before prints were taken and the pictures themselves finished, all of them working day and night debating on the type of frame and mount to suit each picture and Sam had to admit they looked pretty good when they were finished. She was so flattered that they liked them, but she seriously doubted they would sell any. It was, however, very good of them to try.

They advertised an exhibition and it was set for the end of the month. She came home one day after dinner out with

Alberto to find a poster on the door with her name on it and one of her pictures, the old man with the onion and flask of wine, underneath. She couldn't help but feel a thrill of excitement.

They picked a Saturday night for the opening party and ordered two cases of Prosecco. Gianfranco sang as he made up trays of canapés. Everyone on their local client list was invited and came eagerly, Sam thought as much for the free drinks and canapés as for the pictures. She was thrilled too that Giulia had come to help, having said wild horses wouldn't keep her away from seeing her friend's triumph. She was busy setting out glasses while Richard opened bottles and Gianfranco of course was finishing off in the kitchen.

The doors opened and the guests arrived; Sam and Giulia circled the room with trays of drinks and food, listening to the comments and were amazed to find that every single one was complimentary. By the end of the evening there were 'sold' red stickers on seventy percent of them and Richard had orders for a couple of dozen more prints as well.

When the last guest had gone and they all sank down on the sofa in the apartment above the gallery, completely exhausted, Richard leant over and gave her a hug. "Well done, told you so. You are now officially a celebrity artist! There will be no holding you back now. We will have to pay to speak to you."

Sam was so choked up with pleasure she could hardly say anything.

"We will make more prints of all of them and you must have two afternoons a week free to paint more originals."

"Slave driver," Sam laughed, but Giulia hugged her.

"I am so proud of you, my clever friend."

"I still can't believe that people like my work."

"Or that they are selling like hot panini," Gianfranco said. They all laughed.

"Not quite," Richard said, hugging him affectionately, "but that will do."

Chapter 16

Not long afterwards, Sam was in the gallery one afternoon collating a series of sketches by a well-known local artist when she heard Gianfranco calling urgently.

She raced upstairs and to her horror saw her uncle Richard lying prone on the floor with Gianfranco bending over him. "Ambulanza…call an ambulance," he screamed.

"What number?" Sam shouted. She knew 999 in English but in Italy?

"118, 118, quickly," he screamed.

With trembling fingers Sam dialled. She gave the name of the street and added the name of the gallery.

Luckily, she could soon hear the familiar siren of the ambulance which was based a few streets away. She raced downstairs to wait at the door of the gallery and show the paramedics the way. Richard was a dreadful colour and Gianfranco, weeping hysterically, was pumping his chest and shouting to Richard not to leave him. "I knew this would happen," he kept saying. "I knew it! I told him not to eat so much. I kept telling him, but he didn't listen. He didn't listen." He wailed.

The paramedics rushed upstairs and took charge, fitting him with an oxygen mask and then placing him on a stretcher to carry him downstairs into the waiting ambulance, followed by the distraught Gianfranco.

"Look after the gallery, Sam," were the last words Gianfranco said as he disappeared into the ambulance with Richard. The doors closed and it raced away, siren blaring, adding to the general cacophony of the Neapolitan street.

"Phone me," she shouted after the disappearing ambulance, but it was already well out of earshot and she was left alone with total responsibility for the gallery.

She took a deep breath, trying to stop the trembling.

She had difficulty sleeping that night, even after receiving a message from Gianfranco that Richard had been stabilised. He had a heart attack of course, but was receiving good treatment and Sam was comforted by the knowledge that Italian medicine was among the best in the world. Gianfranco was staying with him until he was over the worst.

So, Sam was in sole charge. She opened the gallery as usual the next morning and trade was brisk so she was rushed off her feet. It was a popular spot for tourists to come to, wanting a souvenir of their holiday. Her own pictures with their quirky designs were in much demand and a lot of people asked where the village was with such lovely characters. She was very happy to tell them and hoped she boosted business in the village as a result.

Alberto dropped by in the late afternoon and was horrified to hear what had happened and that she hadn't even had time to eat so he rushed off to buy her a sandwich.

After she closed the gallery he wanted to take her out to dinner, but Sam was worried Gianfranco would come home and find her missing. She was anxious to get news of Richard and also have the chance to visit him once he was out of intensive care.

Sure enough, they were sitting in the kitchen eating takeaway pizza when a clearly exhausted and still very emotional Gianfranco arrived home.

Sam knew enough not to pester him for news too soon, but to let him relax.

Alberto poured the three of them a large glass of wine and they sat on the balcony with the wonderful view of the bay of Naples spread out before them, the sun slowly sinking on the horizon.

She could see Gianfranco slowly unwinding though when she mentioned Richard's name his eyes filled with tears. It appeared Richard's arteries were blocked, several of them and they had inserted four stents to help the flow of blood and avoid more blood clots.

"I knew he was going to be in trouble. I told him so often," Gianfranco kept repeating. "He ate too much, drank too much, didn't take enough exercise. It was bound to happen sooner or later."

Sam was very appreciative of Alberto's help over the next few days, especially as Gianfranco returned to the hospital early the next morning and Sam was once again left in charge. He came every evening bringing dinner for her and for Gianfranco when he returned after a long day sitting at Richard's bedside.

Sam herself was of course very anxious to visit her uncle, but it was only at the weekend on the Sunday when she was able to close the gallery for two days that she persuaded Gianfranco to rest at home before he himself became ill with anxiety and stress.

She arrived at the hospital and made her way through the maze of corridors to the cardiac ward. She passed rooms full of patients being tended to by family and friends. It seemed to be an important part of Italian culture that the family were encouraged to help with washing and feeding once people were on the road to recovery. It certainly freed up the nurses for more important tasks.

She found Richard at last sitting up in bed and looking remarkably cheerful. She kissed his forehead.

"You gave us quite a fright," she said, "but you look better."

"I feel better," Richard responded. "Nearly time to come home. I'm sorry you have had to hold the fort."

"It's no problem." Sam replied. "The main thing is to get you well again."

"They say I've got to watch my diet," he grimaced, "not too many cannuoli."

Sam knew he was particularly fond of those lovely cream-filled Sicilian cakes.

"Yes, yes," she laughed. "It's rabbit food from now on and ten miles along the seafront every day."

He looked crestfallen, but then he brightened a little. "They say wine is good for the heart so maybe it's not all bad news."

"Strictly one glass though and not the whole bottle."

She sat by his bedside, holding his hand. "Sorry again to leave it all to you," he said. "Gianfranco wouldn't leave my side."

"Quite right too," Sam said, "he really loves you."

"I know." Richard smiled. "I am lucky to have found him."

At that moment, the door opened behind her and Richard said, "Good afternoon, doctor. Still on duty? I think you've met my niece?"

Sam turned her head and froze.

It was Federico.

Chapter 17

Did she imagine it or did he flush slightly at the sight of her? He certainly hesitated for a moment and then gathered himself together to switch to full doctor mode.

"Yes, of course. How are you, Sam?" He asked politely.

She smiled and answered equally politely. "Fine thank you."

Then he turned his attention to Richard. "How are you feeling?" He held Richard's wrist, feeling for his pulse.

"A little better, thank you," Richard raised himself off the pillow.

"Do you want me to leave?" Sam asked.

"No, no," he turned to her. "No, don't worry. Just a few checks and I'll be done." He looked at his chart then listened to Richard's heart and gave a few taps on his back. "Good, good, you are definitely on the mend. I'll leave you to your visitor." He smiled at Richard and patted his arm.

He went towards the door, then at the last moment, as if as an afterthought, he turned.

"Goodbye, Sam," he said in a formal manner. "Good to see you again."

Then he was gone.

"Ah," said Richard knowingly, seeing Sam's blush, "Is that how the land lies?"

"Well," Sam replied, trying to sound casual, but finding it impossible to keep the trembling out of her voice. "He's very nice, but I think he's spoken for."

"Mm," said Richard, "that's a pity."

Sam didn't reply.

He was silent for a moment. Then he said. "He likes you though. I could tell. He lost his composure for a moment when he came in and saw you."

Sam felt a tear slide down her cheek which she angrily brushed away. Richard put out his hand and held hers.

"All is not lost in love. Maybe things will change. Love will find a way."

It was Sam's turn to be silent. Then she said huskily "Anyway the most important thing is for you to get better and for us to have you home. Gianfranco misses you. I miss you. Gianfranco isn't singing any more and I never thought I would miss that terrible voice of his, but I do." They both laughed.

They chatted for a little while longer, then she could see Richard was getting tired so she took her leave, kissing him tenderly on both cheeks, adjusting his pillows and tucking the bedclothes around him.

"You'd make a good nurse…and a good mother," he said sleepily and as she quietly closed the door of the room behind her his eyes were already closing.

She went along the long hospital corridor to the main exit. The foyer was still crammed with visitors. Even in hospital, Naples still had the air of a party town. She smiled.

She went out of the main door and down the steps, wondering what to do with the rest of her day.

Then she stopped abruptly because, at the bottom of the steps a familiar figure was leaning on the end of the balustrade.

"Oh," Sam said. "What are you doing here?"

"It's the end of my shift," Federico replied. "I thought you looked tired and might like a little company. It's obviously been a tough time for you. No strings, as I think you say in England. I want to make up for the time in Matera when I didn't behave very well."

"Neither did I," she said. "I overreacted." She took a deep breath and made a decision.

She vowed once again to just enjoy the moment even if it lead to more heartbreak.

"So, shall we walk together?" He said.

"Oh," she said again. "That would be very nice. Where do you suggest?"

"Are you hungry, because I know I am. I will take you for a pizza, but not any old pizza. This is a true Neapolitan one."

Sam realised that she was very hungry indeed. "Sounds wonderful."

They walked together, entering the narrow streets of the old town.

"Where did you learn your English?" She asked. "It's very good."

"Thank you. I suppose I was a good student at school and then I spent one summer at a language school in Windsor. I tried hard to mix as much as possible with English people. The trouble with language schools is that you are nearly always with people from your own country or other people who don't speak English."

Sam laughed. "Several people have told me that. I am very lucky being here in that I can listen to Italian every day so I hope to learn more quickly; and of course, I am forced to learn quickly because many people I meet don't speak English."

It was his turn to laugh. "But you must be careful to learn Italian and not Neapolitan. It's such a strong dialect that many Italians don't understand what the locals are saying."

"Yes, my uncle has already warned me about that." She hesitated. "I know I shouldn't ask because you are a professional, but, my uncle, is he going to be alright?"

"Yes, but," Federico's face was serious for a moment, "he really must lose some weight and get more exercise."

"I know. Gianfranco has been telling him that for quite a while but it won't be easy. He does love his food and wine."

"Talking of food and wine, or food anyway," Federico said, "this is it."

They had arrived outside a very small, unprepossessing-looking shop tucked away in one of the back streets. Federico led her inside and a very old lady, dressed in the ubiquitous black, greeted him warmly. He was obviously a regular visitor.

She was kneading the dough in front of her and she broke off a couple of pieces and flattened them into the two traditional pizza circles. She then took a basin of fresh white, creamy ricotta cheese. "Fresca stamattina" fresh this morning. Sam understood. They watched as she added a piece of strong smoked provolone cheese, a little pork fat and a leaf of basil before folding the whole thing over like a pasty. She placed it in the wood-fired pizza oven behind her and they waited until until the edges were crisp.

"Ecco, here you are." She handed them over, each wrapped in a paper napkin.

"Grazie Nietta." He paid and with a final goodbye, they left the shop and walked along the street munching.

"It's delicious," Sam said, trying not to talk with her mouth full. "I thought I'd tried every type of pizza going, but this is extraordinary."

"It's the oldest recipe for pizza in Naples," he said.

They walked in silence, still eating and when the final crumb was finished he looked at her and said, "Coffee?"

"Yes please."

He was still looking at her and she hoped against hope that he was going to kiss her again, but then he smiled and said "May I?" And leant forward and gently wiped a crumb from the side of her mouth.

"There," he said.

"Thank you."

They turned into the next bar and he ordered and paid for three coffees.

"Are you having two?" She queried.

"No," he laughed. "Here in Naples it's an old custom. One for yourself and one extra for someone who needs it. We are kind-hearted people. We make up our own rules, but we look after those who are, how do you say, down on their luck?"

"That's wonderful. I like that idea." She was touched by the thought. "Where are we going now?"

"Have you seen the Caravaggio in the Misericordia Church?"

"No, I haven't had a chance yet. So many places to visit. It was on my list."

"Well, it's here." They were in front of the facade of a church just round the corner from the Duomo, the cathedral.

"This is a very special church," Federico said. "It's also a charity, a place for concerts and dramas. It was founded in 1601 by a group of young noblemen to help the poor and refugees. The church is full of paintings, but there is one special one."

He took her hand as they entered and it seemed to Sam the most natural thing in the world.

Through the darkness lit only by the flickering candles left as prayers for the dead, Sam could see a massive painting filling the rear of the altar. Federico put money in a slot and a light came on.

She gasped.

"Wonderful is it not?" He was still holding her hand tightly. "Caravaggio came here when he was on the run after he killed someone in a brawl. They commissioned him to paint seven works of art depicting the seven acts of mercy, but he cleverly combined each act of mercy into one painting. The seven acts are, to feed the hungry, heal the afflicted, refresh the thirsty, shelter the homeless, visit the sick, dress the naked, console the imprisoned and bury the dead. The angel at the top is coming down, do you see, to bestow grace on those who show mercy."

They stood in silence, absorbing the beauty of the painting, the light shining on each act.

"Wonderful," Sam said. She was proudly moved.

"Isn't it?"

"You love art then?" She asked.

"Yes, of course." He looked at her in astonishment. "Haven't you already seen that? You think that because I am a doctor I am only interested in things to do with the body? Italy is the home of great art and we as a nation are very proud of that fact. Everywhere you go there are beautiful buildings, sculptures, paintings and frescoes. People ask why there are so many ruins in Italy, but there are so many we don't have the time or the money to restore them all."

"Yes, of course, I didn't mean," she faltered. Then she realised he was teasing her.

"We even have a Warhol and a Banksy. I will show them to you one day."

They left the church and wandered slowly back to the gallery. It had begun to rain and they started to run, laughing. They arrived soaking wet and still laughing.

"Will you come in and get dry?" She said reluctant to let him go.

He hesitated "No, I cannot," he said. A cloud passed over his face. "I have an appointment."

"Oh," Sam said. She was tempted to add "with her?" but bit her tongue.

He turned as if to walk away, then on an impulse, turned again and came towards her. He smoothed the wet hair from her cheek and leant towards her. She closed her eyes expecting a kiss, but it never came. He drew back, his expression anguished.

"I am sorry," he said. "So sorry. I wish things could be different."

Then he turned on his heel again and was gone, vanishing around the corner leaving her staring after him as the rain continued to pour down, echoing the misery in her heart.

Chapter 18

While Richard was in the hospital, Sam was frantically busy. Gianfranco was spending all his time at Richard's bedside so Sam had to do everything, do the shopping, keep the flat clean and run the gallery. Gianfranco was normally the cook of the household and no one else was allowed near the stove except in an emergency. This, of course, was an emergency. Alberto, who had brought suppers the first couple of days, was away on business.

She was subsisting mainly on leftovers and takeaways, but she felt bad that she didn't have a proper meal waiting for Gianfranco when he got home late and exhausted, his face still grey with worry even though Richard was now well on the mend.

They cooked a hasty meal of packet spaghetti, often with just tinned beans from the store cupboard. So, she resolved to get up extra early the next morning and go to the main market, the Mercato de Porta Milano, which was not far from the gallery.

She just had time, if the gallery opened at ten, to be at the gates when it opened at 8am.

She also needed a distraction from her constant thoughts about Federico, the wonderfully relaxed time they had spent together when she had really thought they were building some sort of relationship, then totally spoilt yet again by the way he had said goodbye.

So, armed with a couple of shopping bags, she was standing near the archway supported by two cylindrical towers the locals called Faith and Hope, bearing the crest of Ferdinand the First of Aragon on horseback, the remnant of the old mediaeval city gate. Already at 8am there was a cacophony of noise from the greengrocers, butchers and fishmongers inside who had been up hours before setting up their stalls and taking delivery of their goods.

The gates opened and the stallholders began bellowing their wares. She passed those stalls selling fake CDs and cheap souvenirs and went straight to the fishmongers where she knew Gianfranco shopped. She filled one bag with clams and mussels, determining to do spaghetti alle vongole, pasta with clams. Then the other bag she filled with herbs, fat red tomatoes, peppers and aubergines, courgettes with the flowers still attached. She moved to the cheese stall and bought fresh ricotta and mozzarella, finally bread and a box of sfoglatele which were crisp, literally 'folded' Sicilian cakes filled with chocolate which she knew Gianfranco was particularly fond of.

She could hardly carry the huge load home, but as she hastily put the shopping away and tidied herself up to open the gallery, she was pleased she had made the effort.

She was pleased too, to put into practice all the lessons she had had from Giulia's mother Maria. In Naples, Gianfranco had made it abundantly clear that the kitchen was his domain while Maria had been only too pleased to welcome Sam into her kitchen and show her how some of her specialities were made. Sam had spent quite a few amicable hours watching Maria at work, occasionally helping by chopping and stirring, always making mental notes on how much seasoning she was using, the quantities she never seemed to weigh out because she did everything by eye, the deft way she mixed and blended things. She seemed delighted to have Sam alongside her and Sam felt she was beginning to be treated almost like another daughter. The day Maria had allowed her to help in the kitchen she knew she had really become accepted as part of the family. She could see too how Maria's teaching skills had been passed on to her daughter and even sometimes her sons who she was determined were not going to follow the traditional pattern of waiting for the women to do the work. Her patience was endless when Sam hadn't cut the vegetables, the sofritto, the base for the ragu, finely enough, or had inadvertently put too much seasoning in. She nearly always had a remedy for mistakes.

Maria's meals were fantastic and Enrico often complained jovially that it was a good job that he had to climb the many steps to his office in the square nearly a dozen times a day for exercise or he would put on weight from her excellent cooking.

Maria showed her how to make stuffed peppers and courgette flowers stuffed with ricotta, pointing out that the male flowers were better than the female for this (but don't tell the men!) They made parmigiana, a baked dish of aubergine and cheese; Arancini, rice balls flavoured with Parmesan and mozzarella and endless varieties of homemade pasta including carbonara with egg and pancetta, or with seafood or meat sauces.

The gallery was busy that morning and Sam had no time to even think about what she was going to cook. Thankfully at 1pm she turned the sign around to 'Closed' and she could at last relax for a few hours as she didn't open again until four. It was officially siesta time, but there was no time to rest. Besides, she was fired up with excitement at the thought of all the things she was going to make.

She made herself a quick coffee and salami panino, smiling at the thought of how the English always said 'a panini' which of course was the plural.

She sang to herself as she prepared a parmigiana of the aubergines, layering them with cheese ready to be baked, some stuffing for the peppers for the following day, prepared the water for the pasta and the clams and mussels scrubbed with their beards removed and those already open discarded so they were all ready for cooking. The mozzarella and tomatoes, together with some basil would be a Caprese salad and the ricotta would stuff the courgette flowers. She had enough food for the next few days. Normally, they would have shopped every day, but in the circumstances, there wasn't time.

She realised with shock that it was nearly four, but she had been enjoying all the preparation so much that she just had time to tidy up and slip downstairs to open up.

Once again customers flooded in, but the hours flew by until she could thankfully close the door at 8pm. Gianfranco arrived not long afterwards. He sank into a chair and Sam poured him, and herself, a large glass of wine. It was a while before he could speak, but after a few sips, he visibly relaxed.

"How is he?" Sam asked.

"Much better. They think he might be discharged at the end of the week, but then of course he will have to take time to convalesce," he replied and promptly burst into tears of relief. She could see that during all those days of worry and strain, he had not allowed himself to cry, but now he let it all out and sobbed heartrendingly.

She let him cry, just handing him some tissues when the sobs subsided at last.

She went to put the water on to boil for the pasta, putting in that drop of oil and salt as she had been taught.

The mussels and clams were ready in the fridge and on the side were the courgette flowers ready stuffed, with the flour and salt prepared for frying them.

Gianfranco was at her side in an instant. "What are you doing?" He demanded. Then he stood amazed at the sight before him.

"Sam," he asked, "where has all this food come from?"

Sam explained about her early morning trip to the market.

"But where did you learn to do all this?"

"Giulia's mother, Maria. She has been teaching me."

He had the grace to look a little ashamed. "It should have been me teaching you," he said guiltily. "I'm sorry."

"You didn't have time," Sam comforted him. "Here, help me with the courgette flowers while I get the pasta ready will you?"

So, they stood happily side by side, chatting away, preparing the food and waiting until the pasta was al dente, the seafood and the courgettes were ready and they could sit at the table with a second glass of wine and eat, finishing with the Sicilian cakes.

"We'd better make the most of these," he said. "Once Richard comes home, we won't allow any cakes in the house."

Sam looked at Gianfranco, the strain already leaving his face, and smiled. "Yes, it's going to be starvation rations from now on. Richard's not going to like it. We're going to have to stop him slipping out to buy food."

Gianfranco nodded his agreement. Then he said, changing the subject. "Well, if you want my opinion on the supper, the courgette flowers were good, but I don't know what Maria has taught you. I personally would have put in a little more seasoning."

"I'll remember that." Sam tried not to grin.

"And you said stuffed peppers for tomorrow?"

Sam nodded.

"Well, remember to bake the peppers first before you fill them or they'll be too hard."

"I will." Sam nodded solemnly.

Yes, Gianfranco was back to his usual self and very much in charge of the kitchen. All that remained was to have Richard back home, safe and well and to hear Gianfranco singing tunelessly once more and her little family would be back to normal.

Chapter 19

Alberto mostly worked on buildings in and around Naples, but Sam had learnt that he had a fascinating side-line.

"Have you heard of the one-euro houses?" He said to her one day.

"No," Sam replied. "That sounds too good to be true."

"I will take you to see one on Sunday."

He collected her the following Sunday when the gallery was closed. Richard was now home from the hospital and looking much better. He had lost weight while he was ill, but there was more to lose and he was very downcast at meal times when Gianfranco produced yet another salad or minestrone or a plate of mixed vegetables with the minimum of oil on them.

"But not even a little pasta? Just one or two ravioli?" He said plaintively.

"No, definitely not." Gianfranco said. "You are on a diet and that's that. If you don't stop eating all those cakes and rich food you will end up back in hospital and next time there might not be a happy ending."

"Tyrant," Richard said, but he was smiling fondly as he said it and he did as he was told and Sam left them to it with Gianfranco's awful warbling ringing in her ears. The flat had been so unnaturally quiet during the time Richard had been in hospital and it was wonderful to hear the tuneless singing and to hear them bickering amiably again.

"Where are we off to?" She said as she settled herself in Alberto's car.

"Aah," he said. "Surprise."

They drove off through the outskirts of Naples and took the country road towards the mountains. For a moment Sam thought they were going to the village, but she soon realised they were going in a completely different direction.

Then finally they were winding their way up the hillside and there before her was another traditional village perched on the top, very similar in outward appearance to the one she knew so well. He stopped the car in the village square and the old men playing cards and a black-clad old lady doing her shopping all stopped what they doing and stared. It was then that the comparison with Giulia's village ceased. Everything around them was much more dilapidated and sad-looking.

Alberto took her hand and led her down a narrow street. He stopped in front of a door almost hanging off its hinges and produced a key from his pocket. He turned it in the lock and ushered her inside.

It soon became obvious that the house was not only empty but had been for sometime.

Sam could see in the dim light something that looked as if it had been a stable. There was a manger along one dank wall with hoops where presumably donkeys had been tied up, and a gnarled wooden structure that had presumably been an ox yoke high up on a shelf. The ceiling had partially caved in. Alberto switched on the light on his phone. Behind the first door was a dim narrow hallway leading to a stone staircase and Alberto, taking her hand again and warning her to be careful, led her upstairs to what had obviously been an old lady's bedroom, sitting room and kitchen. An ancient calendar hung on the wall and Sam, peering at it, realised the date was some twenty years before.

As if to confirm that Alberto said. "It's been empty for years, but everything is still here. Clothes in the cupboard, identity cards, family photos and the coffee pot still on the stove."

"Like something out of Sleeping Beauty. Time standing still," Sam said ruefully. "It's so sad."

"Yes, I think that it was someone's grandmother and after she died the family had moved away and they just left the house as it was because no one wanted it."

He flung open the shutters and Sam gasped. There was a similarly spectacular view that she saw from Giulia's balcony, overlooking distant hills and a wooded valley, but this one was even more enchanting with a ruined castle away on the horizon.

"Don't go out," Alberto warned her. "The balcony won't be safe."

"But why is this place in such a bad state?" Sam asked.

"There are hundreds of places like this in villages in the deep south of Italy," Alberto explained. "In the very poorest part of Italy, there was huge unemployment and people have either gone north to the cities or immigrated to places like America. That's why, for example, there is a Little Italy in New York full of Italian families whose ancestors came from this area looking for a better life. Only the old people were left. Giulia's village is lucky. They have renovated the houses, welcomed tourists and done everything possible to keep it alive."

"Yes," said Sam. "I know that Giulia's father as mayor has done as much as he can for the village and that's why Giulia stays to teach there instead of going further afield. She wants to keep the village thriving."

"Yes," said Alberto. "She is a wonderful girl. I do admire her."

Sam looked at him. There was something in his voice that she couldn't quite pin down.

"But one of the local MPs," he continued after a moment's pause, "had the bright idea of offering these deserted houses for one euro to anyone who was willing to renovate them. The proviso was that they had to come and live in the village and, more importantly, bring employment to the locals and breathe life into places like this again. There are snags. Many people want to be able to park outside their house and don't like small rooms, but there are a lot of compensations, the views for one and the peace and tranquillity. Some of the houses are too far gone and there are problems with asbestos, but the majority are sound and there is always the possibility of knocking two rooms into one and putting in proper bathrooms. Of course, one euro is only the start: there are fees to be paid and of course, a lot of work to be done, but there are grants if you complete the work in three years. The houses are mostly solid though and much of the work is cosmetic."

"And that is where you come in." Sam smiled.

"Yes, I've helped with a number of these houses. Everyone is happy to have them renovated and welcome foreigners. Most of the services are still here and the villagers are delighted to see life returning. There is, or can be, a great sense of community as you've seen in Giulia's village."

They wandered out and back to the village square again. It was definitely like going through a place lost in time, pigeons flapping out through glassless windows, stray cats darting through broken walls, the old church with vegetation growing in every nook and cranny. All so sad and neglected.

But the sandstone walls were beautiful, glowing in the afternoon sun and Sam, despite her sadness at the neglect of such an historic place, couldn't help but be thankful for people like Alberto who gave hope for the future, for regeneration.

They drive home in quiet reflection.

"Thank you, Alberto," she said as he dropped her off, "that was such an interesting day. I'm really grateful to you for opening my eyes."

He kissed her before driving away and as she looked after the departing car she mused on how her head really wanted him to be the one, but sadly her heart told her otherwise.

Chapter 20

After that encounter with Federico Sam's mind had been in turmoil. He did care for her, but would it ever amount to anything? He might still choose Nadia.

One thing was certain though, that she had to finish things with Alberto. Everyone loved him, the uncles, all the family in the village, everyone that met him in fact. Everyone except her.

She loved him as a person of course. He was kind, funny, intelligent, everything a man should be, but the feeling that she felt for Federico, that overwhelming passion, just wasn't there. She had hoped that the attraction would grow, but now she accepted the fact that it never would. She would always love him as a dear friend but she had to make it clear to him that it would never be anything more.

How to tell him though without hurting his feelings?

The answer came in a surprising form.

Two weeks after their visit to the house he was restoring he picked her up again.

Alberto was especially cheerful that day, humming to himself as he drove. Sam smiled. She couldn't help but think of Gianfranco, but Alberto had a much better voice.

They had arranged to go to the village together to help with the olive harvest. Not that it was a huge one, but each tiny garden held at least one tree and there was a small communal collection down in the valley which everyone shared. The trees were old and gnarled, often centuries old and there was an equally ancient olive press deep inside a cave in the valley.

They arrived as everyone was gathering together, including Giulia and her brothers. The nets were spread, the trees were shaken and the ripe olives rained down. The fruit was collected and taken to the press where burly men turned the heavy handle and then they moved on to the next tree. Everyone helped and the usual party atmosphere was in full swing.

Sam had learnt early on to appreciate the full-bodied flavour of the first press, the extra virgin oil, unadulterated, unlike so many commercial oils. She had been surprised to learn that in Italy tastings were held with both oil and balsamic vinegar in the same way as wine tastings. The flavour was nothing like the bland oil she was used to in England. Butter was rarely used in these parts; the land wasn't suitable for cattle, therefore very little butter was available locally, so you dipped your bread in a small bowl of oil with a little salt and the taste was wonderful. Now she actually preferred eating her bread that way.

After a morning of helping with the olive harvest, they arrived at Giulia's house where Maria, as usual, was cheerfully rolling the pasta dough. Kisses were freely exchanged on all sides and Sam was immediately allotted the task of slicing the tomatoes and washing the lettuce for the salad. She remembered the early days when she was treated like an honoured guest and wasn't allowed to do anything. Nowadays, she was treated just like part of the family and immediately given a job. She chatted away with Maria as they prepared the lunch, catching up with all the village gossip. Occasionally, there was a word she didn't understand and she had to ask Maria to explain, but on the whole her Italian was pretty fluent now.

Alberto meanwhile had wandered outside and she could hear him talking to Giulia. She could just see them out of the corner of the open window and they were in animated discussion about something. She couldn't hear what they were saying, but she did hear them laughing and their faces were lit up as they gazed at each other.

It suddenly struck her like a bolt of lightening. Of course, that was why Alberto had been especially cheerful on the way up. He was going to see Giulia! And it was quite obvious that Giulia was delighted to see him as well. How could she have been so blind? Something clicked into place. That time in the almost deserted village that he had taken her to. When he had talked about Giulia there had been something in his voice that she hadn't been able to put her finger on, a deep-felt admiration.

It was as if a light bulb had been switched on. Sam realised she was in a triangle, even a square. She loved Federico, not Alberto; Alberto loved Giulia, Giulia loved Alberto, but neither of them could say anything because they were so honourable they would feel, especially Giulia, that they were betraying Sam if they said anything.

She almost laughed. Giulia and Alberto couldn't declare their feelings for each other until she, Sam, made the first move. All she had to do was set Alberto free to declare his feelings for Giulia.

They had a lovely day together, the three of them walking in the countryside after lunch and the attraction between her two friends became more and more obvious. When Alberto helped Giulia over a ditch he held on to her hand a fraction longer than was necessary and he glanced at her so frequently Sam began to feel like the proverbial gooseberry, the unwanted guest at the feast.

He was unusually silent as they drove back down the mountain to Naples. They stopped outside the gallery. Normally, she asked him in to say hello to the uncles, but instead, she said. "Alberto, may I talk to you for a moment?"

"Ah," he said. "I think I know what's coming."

"I like you very much as a friend." Sam said, "but nothing else. I'm sorry."

He went quiet, but she could see he wasn't exactly upset by what she was saying, so her instincts had been right.

"I understand," he said at last. His head was down and she couldn't read his expression. She plunged on, "I think," she said tentatively, "if I'm not wrong, that there is someone else you like very much."

His startled expression as he looked up at her was something to behold. She thought that he actually hadn't realised himself how much he liked her friend.

He began to smile "Thank you, Sam," he said. "You are very, how do you say, percettiva, perceptive."

So, it was done and they parted on good terms, but she could almost see the car bouncing along as he drove happily away.

The next task was to tell Giulia. She phoned the next morning before school opened. "I just want to thank you and your family for another lovely day. Please thank your mother."

"You know she, and we, are always happy to see you."

Then Sam said, as if casually. "I also wanted you to know that Alberto and I have split up. We have decided that we are good friends, but nothing more."

There was a long silence at the other end of the line as Giulia took in the news. She could only imagine her expression, a mixture of relief perhaps…and then joy.

"Oh." She said at last. "I'm so sorry. Have you had an argument?"

"No, no, nothing like that. As I said, we are still very good friends, but for me it wasn't going anywhere in a romantic way. In fact, I think in the end he was quite relieved when I told him because I know there is someone else he likes very much indeed."

Sam paused. There was another silence. Could Giulia be blushing? Finally, Giulia said. "Thank you, Sam. You really are a friend in a million."

So, it was settled and Sam was very happy for them.

Underneath that happiness though was a touch of envy and a sadness that wouldn't go away because her heart still ached for Federico.

**

The next time she saw Giulia face to face, she knew Alberto had been to see her and that they had been out together.

"Thank you, Sam," Giulia said. "I knew I liked him, very much indeed, but I didn't know how things stood with the pair of you. I didn't want to be that awful person who tried to steal her best friend's boyfriend."

"That's good of you to say so." Sam smiled, "and to be honest I knew our relationship wasn't going anywhere, but I didn't know how to end it without hurting his feelings too much. I think in fact he was also trying to find a way to end it with me without hurting my feelings. That day we came together for the olives and then went for a walk I realised there was a real spark between you which made it easier. He's a lovely man. Be happy."

"We will." Giulia said, and there was a certainty in her voice which made Sam realise how deep her friend's feelings already were for Alberto.

Chapter 21

'*At last*,' Sam thought.

It had been weeks since she had been in the village and she was thrilled to be there again.

It had been hectic down the gallery with not only Richard's illness and convalescence, but her pictures were selling like 'hot panini' as Gianfranco would have it, so she was making more prints all the time and even trying to paint a few more originals. They had branched out into making her pictures into greeting cards as well. Richard could only work for a few hours at a time, sitting making up frames.

It was also a daily battle, as they had predicted, to make sure Richard wasn't overdoing things and battle it certainly was as he was constantly at the fridge and store cupboard when he thought they weren't looking, so they had to limit the things they bought. No biscuits, no cakes, no fattening leftovers. If he mentioned casually that he was going for a stroll Sam always went with him to frustrate any intentions he might have to slip into the local pastry shop.

Gianfranco had turned into a tyrant where Richard's diet was concerned, only because he was so worried about his partner's health.

Now here at last was a free Sunday and she was strolling up and down, being greeted by everyone as a long-lost friend. 'L'Inglesina', the English girl, was now part of the village and everyone stopped to say "Hello" and ask how she was. She was so happy to be able to chat with everyone she met. Even some of the dialect words came naturally to her now.

She thought back to the early days when she had caused great amusement when she had either mispronounced words and accidentally said something rude, or confused the endings of verbs making it sound as if she was about to do something when she had already done it which elicited puzzled looks.

She had often complained to Giulia about Italian verb endings.

"You are right. English verbs are easier to remember. But what is very difficult in English is your pronunciation. Cough, bough, through, all spelt the same but said differently."

"Quite right." Sam laughed. "It is the same for us English too. I can still remember having trouble with those at school."

Worst of all for Sam though, were confusing words that were almost spelt alike but were completely different. For a long time, she kept saying 'cane' a dog, instead of 'carne' meat and Giovanni and Tommaso delighted in the confusion as she constantly complimented Maria on her delicious 'roast dog' instead of her delicious roast meat. Nobody bothered to correct her the first few times she mixed them up because they were enjoying the mistake too much.

Since then it had become a family joke as they asked their mother each time Sam came what breed of dog they were eating for lunch.

One day she had made yet another hilarious mistake when she was standing on the balcony of Giulia's house gazing out.

She had made a remark about the wonderful panorama of rooftops. There was a sudden silence, followed by hysterical laughter from the boys, nearly beside themselves with glee.

"What is it? What have I said?" Sam asked, bewildered.

It took Giulia a while to stop laughing and reply. "Sorry, Sam," she had gasped before lapsing into giggles again. "It's just that you said 'tette' with an e at the end instead of 'tetti' with an i."

"What?" Sam said. "I don't understand."

"Tetti with an I is Italian for rooftops," she doubled up again with laughter, "Tette with an e means nipples." What you actually said was "a beautiful panorama of nipples."

Sam flushed scarlet, then she too began to giggle and soon they were all howling with laughter until tears were running down their cheeks.

"Oh dear," Sam said eventually wiping the tears from her eyes with the back of her hand. "I really must be careful. I'm glad I didn't say it in public."

Now as she swung easily up the steps to the main square she nodded and smiled "Buongiorno" or "Ciao" to everyone she met, stopping to exchange a few pleasant words with some, shaking hands with others and enquiring how their son or daughter was doing in faraway cities up north where they had gone to work. She marvelled again at the close-knit community where, it was true that gossip was rife, but where, on the other hand, people looked after each other and no one in trouble was neglected or ignored. She remembered the first few times she had been asked by some of the villagers if she knew their son or daughter who lived and worked say, in Liverpool or Manchester as if they were round the corner from where her family lived and how she had to politely explain that they were in fact quite a long way apart.

She reached the main square at last. On the far side she noticed a little knot of people gathered around a couple she didn't recognise.

Then, in a moment, as someone moved, she saw a figure she did know.

It was Federico and he was standing next to an older woman and man.

Sam stood stock still, gazing.

Their eyes met across the square.

Sam didn't quite know what to do: whether she should go across and greet him or perhaps, she thought, she would be intruding in a private conversation.

She turned to the balustrade and stood looking across at the view of the valley, hardly taking in what she was seeing as her heart was beating so hard.

Then a voice behind her said. "Sam, may I introduce my mother and stepfather to you. Mamma, this is Giulia's English friend Samantha, Sam."

She turned. The elegantly dressed older woman, obviously his mother, as she could see where Federico got his good looks from with those piercing blue eyes, smiled and held out her hand.

"Piacere, Signora," Sam said, shaking her hand.

"I am very pleased to meet you too," Federico's mother said coolly, in perfect English. "Federico has spoken to us about the English girl who has become so much part of the village. He has also shown us your paintings. You are very talented."

Sam was flustered. "I, er, thank you," she said at last, "you are very kind."

There was an awkward pause. Then Federico broke into the silence. "And this is my stepfather Piero."

"Piacere," Sam said again, shaking the hand of the tall, equally elegant silver-haired man in a sharp Armani suit who stood in front of her. At least she put out her hand to shake his, but he took hers, bowed deeply and kissed it in the old-fashioned aristocratic way.

"My mother hasn't been to the village for a long time." Federico said by way of explanation "so she thought she would come and look up a few people, see my father's old home and maybe drop in on Maria if she is at home."

Sam smiled politely. She wasn't sure what Maria would say, aware of her views about the burial of Federico's father, her brother, interred far away down in Naples instead of his home village. Knowing Maria though, Sam was sure she would be politeness itself. She wasn't the type to hold grudges.

The distinguished-looking couple had that city polish which contrasted sharply with the country ways of the villagers. They gave the impression almost of visiting royalty. The elegant woman dressed in the latest fashion stood out amidst the black-clad old ladies and even Sam herself in a t-shirt and jeans.

Federico, too, seemed slightly ill-at-ease while talking to her and Sam noticed his mother scrutinising her son's face, then turning to look at Sam again with the faintest look of puzzlement. Did she detect the emotion Sam was trying to hide? Could she hear my heart beating fast? Sam thought stupidly. Of course, she couldn't.

Whatever she understood there was a sudden froideur in her expression and Sam felt the woman's eyes piercing into her.

"Well," she said at last, "we mustn't stop you from your errand. It was very good to meet you."

Federico's stepfather also bade her a polite goodbye and the three of them moved away to greet some more of the villagers.

Sam gazed after them, feeling slightly humiliated by the encounter as if she'd been dismissed. Then she saw Federico turn towards her. He gave a half smile, shrugged and raised his hand as if in apology.

Then the trio moved down the steps and out of sight.

Sam felt as if she was going to burst into tears. She hastily escaped in the opposite direction down to the old bakery where she had promised to buy the bread for lunch. For a few moments, she was comforted by the sight of the old white-clad baker with his floury hands and the wonderful aroma of freshly baked bread but once she had bought the loaf and was on her way home she had time to think again.

What on earth was going on? She knew that Nadia was Federico's long-term girlfriend and she could only suppose his mother suspected some kind of threat to that relationship for which she must have approved and perhaps even engineered.

If there had ever been any hope of a future with Federico Sam knew now that, with his mother perhaps against her, the situation was even more hopeless. If he was torn between his feelings for her which he had shown her really did exist and his long-term relationship with Nadia, would he ever have the courage to break free?

She was beginning to think that as much as she loved her new life in Italy and how she had hoped to stay, perhaps it was better to leave now, thank the uncles for their hospitality and affection and move on, either back to England or somewhere else. To stay and be constantly faced with the heartbreak of Federico being married to someone else was intolerable. Better to cut loose and try and forget him.

She suddenly felt she couldn't face going back to Giulia's house immediately so, still clutching the warm loaf she walked down to the little cemetery at the bottom of the hill. It was a beautiful spot, not sad at all in a strange way; so peaceful and tranquil, where villagers slept for eternity on the sunny hillside lined with tall cypress trees. There she found a little stone bench among the tombs decorated with the pictures of those who rested there. They gazed at her with unseeing eyes as she wept.

Then slowly she found the peace of that lovely spot infiltrated and soothed her despair and she eventually recovered herself. She washed her face at the tap in the corner and clutching the still-warm bread under her arm she made her way back to the house where lunch was nearly ready.

Giulia looked at her face when she entered. If she noticed something wrong she didn't say anything. Then Enrico came home and announced that he had seen Federico's mother in the village.

Sam could see Maria battling with her feelings, but all she said was "Oh, that's lovely. I hope they come and see us."

This time Giulia did glance at Sam. She had obviously understood something had happened with Federico's mother. Sam looked away hastily before the tears came again.

The three of them arrived at the door an hour after lunch, with many apologies for the lack of notice. "It was a spontaneous decision," Federico's mother said.

The cantucci biscuits and Vin Santo were produced and the room soon grew warm with reminiscences about the old days and people they had known in their youth. Sam, feeling Federico's gaze on her, sat silently in the corner until she could bear it no longer.

She rose and left the room. Giulia's eyes followed her, but she herself felt constrained to stay and help with the visitors.

Sam slipped out of the front door and made her way up the steps to one of the tiny picturesque squares.

It only seemed a moment before she saw Federico come out of the front door, look around, then walk up the steps towards her.

"May I?" He asked, standing in front of her and looking down, his tall figure blocking out the sun.

Sam nodded. He sat down.

"I'm sorry," he said. "I think my mother was a little rude."

Sam said quietly "Maybe she had cause to be Federico," she continued. "I don't know what is going on, but I think you are, as we say in English, playing fast and loose with me. You are obviously with Nadia, yet you think it is alright to kiss me and lead me on. You blow hot and cold with me, encouraging me one minute and then pushing me away the next. Is that just the way Italian men are, stringing girls along to satisfy their egos? I just wish you would leave me alone."

He flushed and was silent for a moment.

"I'm sorry, Sam," he said eventually. "Please give me a chance to explain. It is so complicated. I have known Nadia since we were children together and my mother," he broke off, then began again. "My mother expects." He stopped again, then he said. "It must be difficult for you to understand."

"I thought we had got beyond the age of arranged marriages," Sam burst out.

"Arranged marriages!"

He rose to his feet so abruptly she recoiled backwards, nearly losing her balance.

"What do you think we are?" He shouted, suddenly furious. "That may have been the case two centuries ago, but I think we have moved on a little since then. We are not peasants, you know."

"I never meant that you were." Sam was equally furious "Well, if it isn't an arranged marriage, it really sounds like it. Either that you are the worst mummy's boy I have ever met. If you are such a coward that you can't stand up to your mother, I want nothing more to do with you."

"Mummy's boy? Is that what you think of me? Surely you don't think that?"

He was calmer now. "Please, let me explain."

He sat down beside her again.

"You must understand that when my father died," he paused, gathering his thoughts, "it was just my mother and I for a long time until my stepfather came along. I was the man of the family if you like, even if I was only a boy, and I did everything I could to please her, to make her happy. We were very close to Nadia's family and they were very supportive. My father was her father's best friend and she and I were the same age. We went to school together every day, spent nearly all our time together, celebrated birthdays, Christmas, every special occasion together. We stayed in each other's houses,

153

we ate together, we grew up as teens together and I took her to parties and dances, so it began to be obvious that they all thought we would marry one day. When my father died her father was there to help us and support us and we were so grateful. We owed them so much. I am very fond of her. We get along well together and I just assumed myself I think that one day we would marry. We went along with everyone's expectations, knowing that nothing would give them greater pleasure. But I have never asked her. We are not engaged or anything like that. We just share a common bond." He stopped again and took a deep breath "until there was you."

"Oh," Sam said. "But do you love her?" She shocked herself by the force of her feelings for him, fearful that if he said 'yes' it was all over.

"I thought I did, but then you came along and it feels different, much more overwhelming; and I really, really don't know what to do, how to sort it out without hurting all the people I care about, and that includes you." His expression was one of desperation. She could see he was feeling truly wretched.

Sam felt she couldn't push him any further. In a strange way, she almost felt sorry for him. She was now beginning to understand the weight of expectation on him, but he couldn't marry someone he didn't really love, could he? Even though caring about other people's feelings was what made him a sympathetic and empathetic doctor.

"Well," she said at last, more gently now, "you had better try to sort your life out, hadn't you?" She was tempted to tell him the depth of her feelings for him, but that would have been unfair. She couldn't push him into a decision that he might later come to regret. She could see that his mother was a forceful woman, used to getting her own way and Nadia? Would it break Nadia's heart? Would he live to regret it if he chose Sam and then realised she was only a passing fancy and that his heart really belonged to Nadia? They sat together in miserable silence. He reached out and took her hand and held it.

"Sam," he said, "I have never had feelings as strong as I have for you, but you must give me time. Please give me time."

She noticed that he stopped short of actually saying he loved her and she wanted to hold his hand forever and beg him to choose her. She was restrained enough to know that he had to sort things out for himself, that she couldn't force him.

She withdrew her hand and rose to her feet. She bent and kissed his cheek gently, trying to stop herself from trembling…

"Goodbye," she said. "I hope you make a decision soon. In Bocca al Lupo," she added the old Italian blessing, "In the mouth of the wolf." Giulia had told her about the legend of Romulus and Remus who had been abandoned and then suckled and nurtured by a she-wolf before they grew to manhood and founded the city of Rome. Such a caring saying and full of the emotion she was feeling at that moment.

Then she turned on her heel and walked away, leaving him staring after her.

Chapter 22

The uncles were taking her to the opera. She had never been to one before and was vaguely aware that large ladies and even stouter men stood and bellowed at the top of their voices. Still, it was all an experience and she was game for that.

She put on her best dress and the uncles their suits. Richard adjusted Gianfranco's tie and patted him on the cheek and they were off.

The Teatro San Carlo was a magnificent building attached to the royal palace.

"The king used to have his own private access in the old days, but the original opera house was destroyed by fire and had to be rebuilt. It is still one of the oldest opera houses in the world," Gianfranco told her.

The marbled foyer was crowded as they entered the wide front doors. Sam was amused to see a range of clothing from serious evening wear, the men in tuxedos, the women in full-length evening dresses and flashing their diamonds, down to the young people in jeans and sweaters. She was surprised to see so many youngsters. She had always thought opera was for old people.

"In Italy opera is for all," Gianfranco said. "As a nation we love it. It is in our soul. As you know a great percentage of operas are in Italian. It's such a musical language. And of course, many of the great composers, Verdi, Rossini, Puccini, are Italian as well."

"And Madam Butterfly is one of the best and the saddest," Richard interposed eagerly. "You will love it."

The horseshoe-shaped auditorium took Sam's breath away, decorated as it was all in red and gold with a magnificently frescoed ceiling.

They took their places and Sam felt a stir of excitement. The orchestra pit was full of musicians already and the conductor arrived and took his bow to rapturous applause. The overture began. And so did Gianfranco. He started humming along slightly tunelessly under his breath and Richard tapped him gently on the arm so he stopped. Sam noticed that quite a few of the audience were doing the same or tapping along in time. There was no doubt that Gianfranco was right. Music was in the very soul of Italy.

She was soon totally absorbed in the story of Madam Butterfly and her American lover, Pinkerton, who staged a marriage with her and then sailed away, leaving her pregnant.

They ate ice cream in the interval and Richard ate two, much to Gianfranco's disgust. "You will end up in the hospital again." He grumbled, but Richard just said. "It's my evening off. I diet tomorrow."

The second half with the vigil while Butterfly waited for Pinkerton's return with her maid and little son was so beautiful that Sam held her breath. Not knowing the story, she was aghast when Pinkerton arrived with his new American wife. Tears were already streaming down Richard's and Gianfranco's faces and Richard held Gianfranco's hand as he began to sob quietly.

Then as Madam Butterfly gave her son to Pinkerton and his new wife and finally killed herself, Sam too began to cry. The curtain came down and the singers appeared. "Favoloso!" The applause was thunderous and Richard and Gianfranco were on their feet applauding. Flowers were thrown and the singers took curtain call after curtain call. Shouts of "Bravo! Bravi!" rang out.

"So?" Richard asked as they exited the theatre, still mopping their eyes, "Did you enjoy that? Would you come again?"

"Oh yes," Sam breathed rapturously. "It was fantastic. What a wonderful spectacle; and the music was amazing. But so sad."

"Maybe Rossini next time. Something lighter. No more tragedy."

"Ah, Figaro, Figaro, Figaro," Gianfranco burst out loudly and the crowd around them smiled. They exited into the warm Neapolitan night with stars shining on the water in the bay.

Then Richard said hopefully "Who's for a nightcap and a little snack before bed?"

The snack was firmly vetoed, but they did indulge in a little glass of limoncello before bedtime.

Sam dreamed that night of Japan and cherry blossom, hoping that one day she would get to see it for real. She smiled in her sleep.

Then her dreams were populated by the children from Giulia's school, especially a child whom looked like Madam Butterfly's little boy. The dreams became more feverish as she dreamed of the child she would have with Federico and it being snatched away. Then the tussle between Madam Butterfly and Pinkerton's new wife became the tussle between herself and Nadia for Federico's affection and she cried in her sleep.

She awoke with a start to the smell of coffee and the sound of Gianfranco already preparing breakfast and singing loudly. She showered vigorously, as if to get all traces of her dreams out of her system, then she dressed to begin the new day.

Chapter 23

One day, Maria was unusually quiet.

Sam missed the cheerful chattering and humming that normally accompanied her cooking.

"Is your mother feeling alright?" Sam whispered to Giulia in the hallway "She isn't ill, is she?"

"No, she's not ill," Giulia whispered back. "Today would have been her brother's birthday. She is thinking about him and remembering their life together before he went to Naples. I think they were very close and did everything together. He looked after her and was a truly wonderful big brother. I know she missed that a lot before my father came along and she found true companionship again."

"I'm so sorry," Sam said.

"And of course, she has no grave to visit unless she goes down to Naples. She still thinks he should have been buried here in the family plot. She is such a good person and she tries not to feel bitter, but it is hard for her." Giulia's face was set in a hard expression in her sympathy for her mother.

Sam was silent. Poor Maria, the loss obviously still pierced her heart like a dagger, made worse by the fact of Olivia's lack of compassion for her husband's family.

Then Sam's mind wandered to Federico. Not that he was ever very far from her thoughts. At least he would be able to visit his father's grave and feel close to him. She felt happy that he would have that comfort. Suddenly, despite herself, she felt tears pricking her eyelids and Giulia, thinking the tears of sympathy were meant for her own mother, hugged her in gratitude.

***

It was autumn and time for the Sagra in the village.

Giulia had explained that it was a celebration of local food and towns and villages all over Italy held them.

"Ah, what we call a harvest festival in England," Sam said. "We have a service in church to give thanks that all is safely gathered in and that we have food for the next year."

"Exactly. Well, not exactly," replied Giulia. "It used to be a religious occasion, but now it's just another excuse to have a good time."

"That figures," Sam laughed, "but I didn't think Italians needed any excuse for a party."

"Usually we celebrate one particular dish," Giulia went on "like wild boar, chestnuts, chocolate, mushrooms but tonight we celebrate everything, whatever is in season."

After an early breakfast, Sam had been helping all morning to set up the trestle tables in the main square with paper tablecloths, cutlery and paper cups for the wine. The men, led by Enrico, were erecting the barbecues for the wild boar which would be turned on a spit while Maria and the other ladies of the village were preparing huge mounds of pasta and tomato sauce as a starter, plus the mushrooms to go with the boar and huge slabs of bright yellow polenta. Afterwards, there would be cake soaked in liqueur. There was much to do and the square was buzzing with people chatting and moving about.

The entire village was coming, together with a number of tourists staying in the little hotel. At dusk, the Zampogna players arrived with their bagpipes made of sheep's bladders. They began tuning up. At least that was what Sam supposed they were doing. It sounded more like Gianfranco singing while he prepared supper, more than slightly off-key.

Giulia's brothers were roped in to help too, together with the other teenagers of the village. Giulia nudged Sam and with a movement of her head indicated that Sam should look at Giovanni who was busy helping one of the teenage girls lay the tables. They were both shy and awkward and very self-concious and Giulia and Sam smiled.

"He's been keen on her for a while," Giulia whispered. "Maybe tonight is the night he finally asks her out." She was glowing with love these days, glancing often at Alberto who was busy helping Enrico with the barbecue, but glancing frequently back at her too. Sam was thrilled for them.

Coloured lights had been rigged up in all the houses round the square and as the day began to fade they were switched on. It was magical. People began to arrive and Sam found herself much in demand with a group of English tourists and even a couple of Australians who wanted to know what was going on and they needed her to translate.

"You speak very good English," one of them commented "Where did you learn it?"

"That's because I am English," Sam laughed.

"Oh, we thought you were Italian. You look Italian and we saw you chatting away with the locals in Italian."

Sam explained that she was working in Italy at her uncle's gallery. "You must come and see it if you are down in Naples." She thought she might as well drum up a little business for the gallery while she could.

"She's being modest," Giulia interjected. "She's actually a very good artist. You should see her pictures."

They all looked at her with new respect.

Everybody sat and the food service began. It was frantic and Sam and the others were kept busy running backwards and forwards, making sure everyone had bowls of pasta and sauce and plenty of Parmesan cheese. The brothers were serving the local wine with, it had to be said, the odd surreptitious glass or two themselves despite the disapproving glare of their mother stationed behind the massive pasta saucepan the size of a beer barrel. She was surrounded by the other women of the village who had also been busy for the last few days preparing the food.

Sam and the others didn't have time to sit themselves because no sooner had they finished serving the last person it was time to clear the plates of the first people to be served and then start serving the main course.

The Zampogna players played faster and faster, also fuelled by frequent glasses of wine.

Then they began to give out the plates of wild boar, cooked by the men on the barbecues, with the ladies doling out the mushrooms and polenta. The noise by this time was deafening between the shouting and clapping and the bagpipes and the smoke from the barbecues was getting in her eyes.

She blinked to clear them as she put the plates in front of two people sitting in front of her. She saw with a shock that it was Federico. And next to him was Nadia.

She nearly dropped the plates as her knees went weak. Nadia looked up and said "Oh hello, Sam. Good to see you."

Federico looked up too and it wasn't just her imagination that he looked distinctly uncomfortable, but it was hard to tell in the dark.

"I persuaded Federico to bring me to the village to see what was so wonderful about it that brought him here so often and this is such fun. You are working hard I see. Really like one of the locals."

"Yes, I've been roped in by Giulia." Sam tried to sound calm "but I love being here with all my friends." There was a pause and then she said, "Well, good to see you both enjoying yourselves. I must keep on working or people will be complaining that they are not getting their food."

She walked away, trembling.

It was bound to happen, she thought miserably. Nadia is staking her claim on him and making sure I know it.

She got through the rest of the service in a daze, removing the empty plates and then serving the cake. When they finally cleared up the rest of the dirty plates and cleared up the rubbish Giulia said "Wow, at last we can eat something. I'm starving! Come on."

"I'm not really hungry." Sam told her.

"Really? I'm ravenous. It's been hard work," and she went off to fetch a plate of boar. She also came back with two glasses of wine. "Here," she said to Sam, "at least have a drink."

Sam gulped it down almost in one go in an effort to drown her sorrows.

The food finished, the tables were packed away and the singing and dancing began. Old and young took to the floor. A ninety-year old danced with his three year-old great-granddaughter, solemnly placing her feet on his as he led her in a stately fashion around the floor. At any other time it would have been an enchanting sight, but now she could only watch miserably as Giulia and Alberto took to the floor, so obviously besotted with each other. Then she felt sick as Federico and Nadia began to dance, his arm around her waist, she nuzzling his chin with her head. She felt like running away but sat with a determinedly fixed smile on her face.

She was immensely grateful to one of the tourists who came up and asked her to dance and by chatting to him and answering his questions she was at least distracted from the sight of the two happy couples.

Then the singing began. All the old Neapolitan songs which everyone joined in enthusiastically. Then one of the Australian tourists went up on stage and began to sing 'Waltzing Matilda' and all the English speakers joined in lustily, much to the bemusement of all the Italians.

"But what is this word Bill…a…bong?" She heard one of the bewildered Italians ask of her neighbour who merely shrugged in reply as if everything foreigners said were peculiar to her, but soon they were joining in the chorus in a variety of strange accents and Sam could only smile weakly.

Life in the village was always a consolation, however much your heart was breaking.

Chapter 24

Sam's parents had arrived the day after Boxing Day. It was the first time they had been to Italy and the first time they had seen Sam for nearly a year. They had expected her back in England for Christmas and were disappointed that she hadn't gone home, but after a quiet autumn following a busy summer rush of tourists, business had built up again and with Richard not fully up to strength and working shorter hours in the gallery, they had asked her to stay on.

She had broken the news to her mother and could sense she was really disappointed so Sam had said.

"Why don't you come out here for New Year? It promises to be fun and the weather will still be acceptable, well above freezing, warmer than England anyway." She knew her mother hadn't wanted to come in the height of summer because it would have been too hot, but at this time of year it would be ideal.

Sam and the uncles spent Christmas according to tradition. No meat on Christmas Eve, just a bowl of spaghetti with clams, then minestrone, chicken and a little Panettone on Christmas Day. "No seconds, Ricardo!"

Her parents didn't need to be asked twice. They jumped at the chance. As an added bonus they brought their six-year-old granddaughter Becka, the daughter of Sam's brother, Tom.

Sam met them at Naples Airport and surprised herself at the sudden rush of emotion she felt at seeing her parents again after nearly a year. In truth, although they had spoken frequently on the phone, she had been so immersed in her new exciting life that she hadn't thought about them as much as she should have. She suspected that life had always been like that, the parents missed their children when they flew the nest, more than the other way around.

But now, as she hugged her mother and then her father and held Becka's hand as she took their suitcase, she really was glad to see them. Even more than that she was excited to be able to show them the wonders of Italy, to take them to fun places and introduce them to all the new people she had met and especially take them up to the village where Maria and Enrico were anxious to meet them.

First of all, they visited Richard and Gianfranco and brother and sister hugged each other, both commenting how the other hadn't changed a bit while privately thinking that the other had in fact changed quite a lot. It had been quite a few years since they had seen each other. Sam had told her parents that Richard had been in hospital, but had played down the fact that he might have died if it had not been for Gianfranco's prompt action in getting help and the excellent care he had received in the hospital. He was looking a lot better and, although he was still portly, he had lost quite a bit of weight due to regular long evening walks along the Lungomare and a better diet; or what Richard termed 'forced marches and starvation rations'.

They had supper together and Sam noted with a smile her father cutting up the pasta in the way that the Italians had expected her to. She asked after her brother and the other members of the family and talked animatedly about the village and life in Naples, all the interesting things she had seen and done.

She caught her mother smiling.

"What is it?" She asked.

"It's you. I think you are more Italian than the Italians." Her mother laughed. "You talk with your hands."

Sam realised that in fact it was a habit she had picked up without realising. "You will soon see," she said, "that there is even a sign language here in Naples, like a tic tac man at the races, where people can have a whole conversation without words. And there are gestures like putting your hand palm down under your chin and flipping it out which shows you don't care or 'go away' or turning a finger in your cheek to signify that something is good or beautiful. It's fun to watch."

Supper over, she could see both Richard, still not totally recovered, and her parents after their journey, were getting tired so she took her parents back to the little pensione they were staying in around the corner. Becka though, was staying with her, in a camp bed in the corner of her room and Sam was delighted to have her. She was an intelligent child and full of personality.

They talked long into the night with a rather over-excited Becka asking question after question about life in Italy. It had been the first time she had been on a plane, her first time abroad and she was fizzing with energy. She mentioned at one point the pannacotta roofs which had Sam puzzled until she replied, trying not to laugh, that they were terracotta as in baked earth, not pannacotta as in baked cream. Eventually, it really was time for Becka, and Sam, to sleep and Sam said, "Nighty, nighty."

"Pyjama, pyjama," Becka said.

Sam laughed. It was an old family tradition and she was glad her brother and sister-in-law had kept it up...

"Don't forget the other ones," Becka said.

"You mean 'Go to sleep you ugly little monkey, I'll hit you with a hammer if you don't. You think you'll get some supper because you had no dinner. Bet you half a dollar that you don't?'"

"Boom, boom," they chorused together gleefully.

"And the other one," Becka begged.

"Ah you mean 'Nite, nite, sleep tight, don't let the bed bugs bite'."

Becka squealed with delight. Then she asked. "What do the Italians say?"

"Well, certainly nothing like those. It's 'Sogni d'oro', dreams of gold. I suppose it's a bit like our 'Sweet Dreams'."

"Oh, much nicer in Italian." Becka said sleepily and with that she closed her eyes and was immediately in the land of Nod.

Sam lay watching her innocent face in repose for some time before finally drifting off to sleep herself.

Becka of course was up early the next morning, dragging Sam out of bed and asking eagerly where they were going that day. The gallery was shut for a few days for the post-Christmas period so Sam was taking Becka and her parents sightseeing.

After breakfast, they left Richard and Gianfranco in peace, but Gianfranco was already preparing a sumptuous

169

feast for the evening. She and Becka went round to fetch her parents from the pensione. It was several days until New Year, but the Christmas markets were still in full swing and would be so until Epiphany so Sam had promised to show them around.

Becka skipped along beside Sam, holding her hand. She was very excited because Sam had told her all about the Befana who, in Italy, comes on the 6th of January, bringing presents for the children.

"Do you mean I get more presents?" Becka said, her eyes wide with glee. "As well as those I got for Christmas?"

"Well, if you are very, very good that may be possible. In Italy children get some presents after lunch from Babbo Natale, Father Christmas, and more at Epiphany. You know that is when the wise men brought presents to baby Jesus."

"But who is the Befana?" Becka asked…

"She is a very old, very ugly witch who arrives on her broomstick."

"Oh," Becka said. "Well, she can't be a nasty witch if she brings presents."

"No, I've been told it's because she was too late to see the baby Jesus herself so she brings presents for the children instead. But," she added, putting on a mock stern expression, "you have to be very, very good or you get a piece of coal instead because that's what the naughty children get."

"Can I choose my own presents?" Becka said, undeterred.

"We'll see about that." Sam laughed.

"I'm going to live in Italy if you get two lots of presents." Becka said decidedly, "Much better than in England."

They had arrived at the San Gregorio Armeno market place and Sam explained to her parents that this was where the Christmas market was held every year from the 8th of December, the festival of the Immaculate Conception, through to the 6th of January.

What a sight met their eyes. They went through streets decorated with lights, music issuing from every open window. "You will have to be careful on New Year's Eve," Sam warned them. "The old custom in Italy was to throw things from the window; all the old stuff you don't need, to say goodbye to the old year. It's not as bad as it was apparently. Uncle Richard said he was nearly hit by an old sofa one year, but some people still hang on to the custom and you don't want to be hit by a flying saucepan. Much better to stay home."

"Quite," her mother said.

"The other local custom they tell me is that it is lucky to wear red underwear."

"What, even me?" Her father said, amused.

"Don't worry Dad, I've already bought you a pair of snazzy red pants." Sam laughed.

"Thanks," he said dryly.

Her mother took the chance, when Becka had skipped ahead, to ask Sam if they were going to meet Alberto, her boyfriend.

She looked crestfallen when Sam explained that he was now with Giulia.

"So Giulia took him away from you? That doesn't sound like a very nice friend."

"No, no, quite the reverse," explained Sam. "He's a very nice man and I like him very much as a friend, but nothing more. I could see that he and Giulia really liked each other so

I ended it with him. I wouldn't be surprised if they weren't engaged any day now."

"Right," said her mother, "as long as you weren't upset. I suppose it's alright. Then if you haven't got an Italian boyfriend you might come home one day. I suppose there's no one else?"

Sam went quiet and her mother stopped, causing the couple behind to almost cannon into them.

"So, there is, is there?"

Sam stared resolutely ahead "No, of course, there isn't. No one available that is."

"He's not," her mother paused dramatically with a horrified expression "married, is he?"

"No, he's not married, but there's a long--term girlfriend. But don't say anything, please." Sam continued. "I don't want people gossiping. I'm just getting on with my life and trying to forget him."

"Oh darling, I'm so sorry," her mother said squeezing her hand.

At that moment Becka bounded up and Sam was grateful that the conversation was at an end. At least she hoped her mother wouldn't ask for any more details.

They were now into the very heart of San Gregorio Armeno, the oldest neighbourhood of Naples. It was known by everyone as the art quarter of the city, but at Christmas time it was especially busy selling nativity scenes, the Presepi, which Gianfranco had explained was a more ancient tradition than having a Christmas tree in Neapolitan houses.

"Jesus, of course, isn't put into the scene until Christmas day," Sam explained as they admired the terracotta figures.

"Not pannacotta," Becka said firmly, which made everybody laugh.

The scenes in front of them consisted not just of the holy family and a few animals with the traditional shepherds and wise men, but also managed to include a housewife cooking spaghetti, electric-powered windmills lit up by tiny lanterns, fountains and waterfalls which actually looked full of water, and a whole zoo of animals including everything that could possibly have fitted in Noah's ark, including zebras and elephants.

Becka was enchanted. And not only Becka.

"Look at this." Sam's father exclaimed. He was looking at the entire football team of Naples, including Maradona. There were models of other famous footballers including English ones, and a whole shelf of politicians of every shape, size and era. And of course, the Pope himself.

Her mother distracted Becka while Sam secretly bought a selection of animals to give to Becka from the Befana. She was just paying for them and secreting them in her bag when a voice behind her said, "Ciao, Sam, what are you doing here?"

She whirled round and there was Federico. With Nadia of course, who else? She was clinging possessively to his arm. Her hand clung even tighter as she gazed at Sam and said "Hello."

"I, I, er," Sam stuttered. "I'm here with my parents. They've come over from England to stay for a week."

"Well, we must meet them. Will you introduce us?" He said.

Sam turned and made the necessary introductions. "Dad, Mum, this is Giulia's cousin Federico and his er, friend, Nadia. Federico, Nadia, my parents."

"Signora, signore, how do you do? I am very pleased to meet you." They shook hands politely.

"And this," Sam said, glad to be distracted, "is my niece Becka, my brother's daughter."

"Ciao," Becka said importantly, being proud of the fact that she knew how to say hello in Italian.

Federico smiled "Ciao Becka," he said, solemnly shaking her hand. Then he continued, "Well, we must buy you a present from the Befana. Which one would you like?" He said, pointing to the array of figures.

Becka hesitated, but only for a moment. Sam hoped she wouldn't be too greedy and was relieved when she chose only the smallest lamb.

"Are you sure?" Federico asked, "Nothing else?"

Sam could see Becka was struggling, but she was a well brought up child and she shook her head. "That would be very nice." she said. Federico went inside to pay then returned with the package and gave it to Becka who thanked him. He also surreptitiously gave Sam another larger package and when Becka wasn't looking he whispered, "For Becka too from the Befana."

"Thank you." Sam said, trying to be polite. She looked directly into Federico's eyes, challenging him. He returned her gaze and held it for a few seconds.

If her mother had noticed her daughter's reaction and put two and two together, she didn't say anything.

Federico and Nadia eventually moved on after Becka had managed another "Ciao."

"Now," Sam asked. "What about a cappuccino for the adults and a milkshake for Becka?"

"Cappu…ci…no," said Becka, proud of the fact that she had learnt another Italian word, spreading her arms wide and enunciating every syllable clearly.

They sat at the cafe, sipping their drinks. Her father was consulting his guidebook. He smiled.

"What is it?" Sam asked.

"It says here that this is a suggestive angle."

"Yes, I've noticed there are lots of suggestive angles in Italian guidebooks." Sam laughed. She had recovered her composure after the encounter with Federico and Nadia and was determinedly planning ahead as to where to take everyone later on.

"More suggestive angles?" Her father laughed…

"Quite possibly," she giggled in reply. "There are a lot of them in Naples. Aside from suggestive angles, the biggest nativity scene is in the national museum."

"Yes," her father said, reading from the page. "162 people, 80 animals and 450 objects. Maybe though the museum is a step too far for Becka."

"Talking of steps too far," her father continued, "I'm getting a little footsore."

"Shall we have an early lunch then?" Sam suggested.

"Pizza!" Becka shouted…

So, pizza it was and of course, afterwards, Becka was dazzled by the number and variety of ice creams, taking an age to choose "Gel…at…to," she said slowly, adding another Italian word to her vocabulary. She couldn't make up her mind.

"Why don't you have three flavours in one cone?" Sam suggested. "That might make it easier."

Becka's eyes lit up. "Can I?"

So, three flavours it was and Becka finished hers with a satisfied sigh. "I'm really, definitely, absolutely, coming to live in Italy," she said. "That was fantastic!"

Sam, seeing her parents wilting, suggested that a siesta might be in order.

So, they made their way back to the pensione and Sam arranged to collect her parents for dinner with Richard and Gianfranco at the gallery.

While Becka was showing her lamb to Gianfranco who was busy chopping vegetables in the kitchen to the tune of 'O sole Mio', Sam hid her parcels in her bedside cabinet. Strangely, there was a very small extra little package which she was sure she hadn't bought. She unwrapped it carefully and there was a little model of the house of the tragic poet in Pompeii wrapped in tissue paper. But who had put it there? Was it a mistake? There was only one possible explanation. Federico.

For a moment her heart sang. Then in a moment, she was plunged into the depths of despair again. She was furious. How dare he! And in front of his girlfriend too. He was trying to have his cake and eat it, or as Gianfranco would have put it, having his panino and eating it. Her laugh had an hysterical tinge to it and her eyes filled with tears that she angrily brushed away with the back of her hand.

She slept fitfully that night, especially after the huge meal Gianfranco had prepared. Her dreams were broken by visions of Federico, but Nadia kept coming into those dreams and snatching him away.

She drifted off into a deep sleep at last and then awoke with a start to find Becka standing by her bed, shaking her.

"What are we going to do today?" Becka demanded.

Sam groaned. "Well, let me wake up properly. Then we'll have some breakfast and decide on a plan of action. I'm sure it will include gelato though!"

"Yippee!" Becka shouted.

"There are of course the fireworks tonight." Gianfranco said as they ate their morning pastries and drank their morning coffees. Becka had a special 'coffee' a 'babycino' which was all frothy milk which she loved. "They will of course be at midnight. Too late for little girls."

Becka looked distraught. "Can't I stay up?" She pleaded.

"We will have to ask granny and grandpa, but I expect they would say that if you have a rest this afternoon you might be allowed to stay up."

"And of course, you will have to watch the fireworks from the balcony here. It's far too dangerous to go out walking on New Year's Eve," said Richard.

"Yes. I've already told them about the things being hurled from windows."

"Quite but there are also always a few idiots lighting fireworks in the street and throwing them around. We will have the best view from the balcony anyway."

After breakfast, they collected Sam's parents from the pensione and they strolled along the Lungomare with its wide vista of the bay of Naples, with boats bobbing on the water, the sun glistening on the white tops of the waves. They exclaimed at the distant view of Capri and admired the seventeenth-century fountains.

"I had no idea Naples was so beautiful," her mother said.

Far away was the towering sight of Vesuvius. "Is it safe?" Her mother asked.

"Hopefully, though you never know. They will apparently give us fair warning if it is due to erupt." Sam said, but she couldn't help thinking of that day in Pompeii with Federico. She immediately suppressed the memory very firmly.

Other people were walking and it was good to get away from the narrow crowded streets of the main part of the city. To the south was the Amalfi coast.

"Next time you come, we will go out along the coast or maybe even to Capri," Sam said.

"That would be lovely," her mother replied. "I'd love to come back. It would be good to see some of the art galleries too. I hadn't realised what I was missing all these years!"

"Oh yes, there are wonderful works of art in Naples. And if Becka comes she and I will go out somewhere else because she would get bored. The Castel Nuovo, the new castle over there," she pointed, "has some lovely pictures too."

They had also seen Richard and Gianfranco's gallery of course and had been astonished to see Sam's work on display as well.

"They are selling really well," said Richard proudly.

"Darling, that is wonderful. We knew you were good, star of your year at college, but had no idea you were this good. What a clever daughter we have." They both hugged her and Sam gave them one of the pictures to take home, a Neapolitan scene to remind them of their visit.

"Think of me when you look at," she said.

"We always think of you, but this will be something special to show the neighbours and boast about our celebrated daughter!" her mother laughed.

They stopped for coffee and to 'people watch' as Sam liked to call it. She found endless inspiration for her painting just by observing little groups chatting and going about their daily business.

Then Becka announced, "I'm hungry."

"What! After all those cakes you had for breakfast!" Sam laughed.

"Can we have pizza again?" Becka pleaded.

So pizza it was, for Becka at least, but Sam persuaded her parents to try some of the more unusual pasta sauces. She showed her parents a little cafe she had discovered and even on New Year's Eve the ladies of the establishment were hard at work making orecchiette.

"Guess what that means." Sam said to Becka.

She screwed her face up and gazed at the little round pieces of pasta which the ladies broke off and flattened with their thumbs.

"Well," Becka said, "they look a bit like little ears!"

"Exactly," Sam said. "You are a clever girl. It's exactly what orecchiette means, little ears."

Becka beamed with pride.

True to her prediction, her parents said Becka could stay up until the fireworks as long as she had a rest in the afternoon, so after lunch, they wandered back home past the workmen busily assembling stages for the evening concerts to be held at various points in the city, with musicians practising in corners.

Her parents safely installed back at the pensione, Sam told Becka to go to bed for a rest which she obediently did, albiet only after Sam said. "If you don't lie down, the Befana won't come at Epiphany with her presents."

While Becka rested Sam helped Gianfranco prepare the evening meal, laying the table and polishing the glasses. Bottles of Prosecco were chilling in the fridge and Gianfranco had made a homemade panettone, rich in dried fruit, together with little stuffoli, small marble-shaped honey balls, for dessert...

It promised to be a gargantuan feast and Richard was already prowling, having his hand slapped affectionately as he tried to reach out for one more of the stuffoli.

They gathered together to eat later that evening and Sam watched contentedly as her two families chatted animatedly.

At the stroke of midnight, the clamour started: shouting, singing, the banging of pots and pans from every side. Becka had already rushed out onto the balcony and they all followed just as the fireworks began along the Lungomare. And what fabulous fireworks they were too. They 'Oohed' and 'Aahed' at each explosion and Becka was beside herself with glee at each new combination of colours.

Sam though couldn't help wondering where Federico was spending his New Year. With her, obviously. She thought nostalgically of that magical evening when they had danced closely in the village, the evening when he had rushed off abruptly and then those fireworks that had gone disastrously wrong with the hillside catching fire.

New Year should be a time for new hope and new beginnings, she thought and she tried hard to shake off that feeling of gloom and despair that hung over her.

She was not one to brood for long though and the mood of depression passed as she concentrated hard on giving her parents a good time.

Maybe this would be the year when things would go well after all.

There was always hope.

Chapter 25

Giulia's father insisted on taking them all up to the village: uncles, parents, Sam and Becka.

Her parents stipulated that they would come only if Giulia's family would be their guests at the little hotel down the hill in return for all the hospitality that they had shown to Sam.

There was a very polite verbal tussle over the matter with Enrico insisting it was their village so they must host lunch and her parents being adamant about returning all the hospitality. They gathered at Maria and Enrico's house for drinks first.

"So this is where you have been spending so much time," Sam's mother said. "It's enchanting." She was looking out at the view from the balcony.

She turned and hugged Maria. "Please tell her Sam that we are so grateful for making you feel so at home."

Sam translated.

Maria reached and put her arm around Sam's shoulders.

She squeezed Sam's cheek and said, "She is very special to us. We love her very much."

Sam's mother looked at Sam enquiringly, but Sam had to swallow hard she felt so emotional.

"She's just being very kind," she replied.

"I'm sure she said something very nice about you," her mother smiled.

"Bella, bella," added Maria, again squeezing Sam's cheek.

"That I did understand," her mother laughed. "She is very beautiful."

Her parents had finally won the day as to who was to pay for lunch so all of them, dressed in their best, assembled in the village square and walked down to the restaurant. Sam's father was unusually tall and Sam smiled at the sight of him escorting Maria, all five feet of her, down the hill, holding her arm in the crook of his, with Giulia walking alongside them translating madly.

Equally, Sam was translating for her mother and Enrico, also walking arm in arm. Becka was skipping along behind them entranced by the lady with the donkey bringing the wood down the steps.

Any initial shyness soon disappeared and with the help of quite a few glasses of the local wine, the room was filled with laughter and much cheering as 'Buon Anno', 'Happy New Year', was wished to one and all with increasing frequency. Becka, not to be left out, was allowed a very tiny sip of wine which she pronounced disgusting and was thereafter very happy with lemonade. Alberto was also present and Sam noticed her mother watching the two of them together. "You can see how much in love they are," she whispered to Sam. "You did the right thing."

Her parents adored the village and puffed obediently up and down the steps, admiring every 'suggestive angle' as Sam's father reminded her with a grin.

At the end of the afternoon, there was much kissing and hugging with promises to come back soon.

Altogether the holiday was a great success and Sam, although sad to see her parents go, knew they would come again before long. They had even promised to set to it and learn some Italian before their next visit.

At the departure gates Becka threw herself at Sam, "I don't want to go," she wailed. "I want to stay with you."

The Befana had brought her a whole load of presents, both from Sam and her parents and also the uncles as well as the extra surprise from Federico.

"You have to go to school," Sam said. "Anyway, you can tell all your friends about your lovely Christmas holidays. I'll bet none of them have had a holiday in Italy with real Italians. You can tell them about the Christmas markets, the fireworks and the lovely village you went to."

"Yes!" Becka's face lit up at the thought of being the queen of the classroom and as the three of them were through the gates and almost out of sight she turned to Sam and shouted at the top of her voice "Ari…ver…der…ci!" Flinging her arms wide and making all the departing passengers smile.

I will miss her, Sam thought, and she already had an idea for the next picture she would paint: Becka unwrapping her presents from the Befana with a tiny image of the Befana watching her while riding on her broomstick and smiling her crooked smile.

Chapter 26

Shortly after her parents left an excited Giulia told her that she and Alberto were engaged.

Sam was genuinely thrilled for her and very honoured when Giulia asked her not only to help her with preparations for the wedding but also to be her maid of honour.

Maria and Enrico too were delighted with their new son-in-law-to-be. He got on so well with all the family and he was already treated like a son. The two families had met and his family approved of Giulia so a happier crowd of people couldn't be found anywhere.

Sam had been in Italy for over eighteen months by now and it felt like home. She knew she would have to go back to England to visit at some point, but as long as the uncles would have her she wanted to stay in Italy. She loved everything about Italy, the buzz of it all where life seemed to be lived to the full with enjoyment in every detail. She had changed her mind and decided that whatever happened with Federico she would have to accept it, but he was not going to ruin her life, the life she enjoyed. Her career was flourishing and she continued to be more and more inspired in her paintings.

Soon it was Easter and the gallery was closed for the weekend, so of course she was in the village.

The previous week she had been in the school with Giulia helping the children make Easter cards for their parents and grandparents and painting eggs. She had also taught them all the English words associated with Easter.

"Eggs," they had chorused, 'rabbits', 'yellow, hot cross buns', 'chicks', 'chocolate'. Especially the latter.

She and Giulia had hidden small chocolate eggs around the classroom and playground and they had had an Easter egg hunt. Sam was worried that Alfredo would be left behind in the hunt, but he proved surprisingly adept and actually found more than anyone else. His little brother was growing fast and when the school day finished she saw him in his pram when his mother came to fetch Alfredo. The children all poured out of the school excitedly showing the cards they had made and eggs they had painted to their parents and Sam and Giulia wished everyone a Happy Easter.

Giulia heaved a sigh of relief at the thought that she would have a short break although there was of course, still a great amount of preparation to do for the following term.

"No peace for the wicked," she exclaimed to Sam as she locked up the school and they walked home.

After lunch, Sam and Giulia went to pay an Easter visit to Giulia's great-grandmother, Nonna Irene, who lived in an adjoining house together with Enrico's younger sister Teresa and her family.

Sam had met her before of course, but at every visit she seemed more frail, her skin translucent, her hair snow white. She was 102 and Sam had marvelled constantly at how many people in the village lived to such a great age.

"The famous Mediterranean diet, oil, vegetables, everything fresh and organic," Giulia had laughed.

"Nowadays the 'Cucina Povera', what you might call the 'poor man's' cooking, has become quite fashionable, but it was a way of life poor people lead because there was very little in the way of meat or dairy in the old days. You ate what you could grow in your garden. And fish of course, if you were near the sea."

Sam had eaten Panzanella quite often, a bread and tomato salad spiced with onion that was a favourite even among people who could afford meat and she had found it delicious. "Not only the diet but hard work without any modern conveniences," Giulia said.

"And not to mention climbing those hundreds of steps every day," Sam laughed.

"Quite," said Giulia. She was holding her grandmother's hand and telling her all about her preparations for the wedding. The old lady was nearly blind and rather deaf and she was tracing the shape of Giulia's face with the other trembling hand.

While they talked, Sam gazed around her. The kitchen was almost identical to the one next door with an old wooden table, a dresser full of odd china, old photos and a crucifix on the wall. On the hearth stood an old heavy metal iron which Giulia had explained that Nonna Irene had used before electricity came to the village.

"She had two, each filled with hot coals and when one cooled down you used the other."

"But it's so heavy," Sam had exclaimed when she first saw it. "I can't believe she actually used this. Especially filled with hot coals."

"Yes, and when electricity was installed my mother had to show her how to use a modern iron and stop her trying to put bare wires into the socket."

"Ouch," Sam said.

"Quite."

Sam had also met Nonna Irene's grandson Matteo, Giulia's cousin, who was in the army and had never risen through the ranks.

"He's a sweet chap, very amiable, but not the brightest," Giulia had laughed. "There are many stories about him but the one I love most is when he was drilling a crowd of recruits standing in line and shouting left right, left right and when one raised the wrong leg, left instead of right he shouted. Who is that idiot with both feet off the ground?"

"Understandable," Sam grinned.

"Then there was the time the captain asked him to bring him the plan for the caserma, the police station. As you know the word for plan and plant are quite alike so I suppose he could have been forgiven when he dug up the tree outside and struggled in with all the mud and stones attached and plonked it on the captain's desk."

After a while, they could see that the old lady was tiring. Giulia kissed her tenderly on both cheeks, wrapped her shawl around her shoulders and then they tiptoed away.

They slipped back into Giulia's house where as usual Maria was hard at work in the kitchen. She was shouting at the brothers to stop eating the chocolate eggs they were supposed to keep for Sunday. "You won't have any appetite for lunch," she said sternly, espying their chocolate-smeared faces.

"I doubt it," Giulia said. "It's nonstop feeding in this house, especially when the boys are home. Normally they eat in school at midday but they are always ready for another meal when they get home. Our Easter holidays are short because we have such long summer holidays in the hot months so they seem to still get through an enormous amount of food. My mother has to keep the Columba, the dove-shaped panettone we have for Easter, locked away or they would start on it."

"Hollow legs, as my mother used to say about my brother Tom when he was a teenager." Sam said. "I remember it well. He grew half a metre in six months and never stopped eating."

"Of course, never quite filled up."

Not only was Maria preparing lunch for that day, which was comparatively modest as it was Good Friday, but she was cooking a ricotta cake for Sunday when her sister's family were coming round as well and preparing several large joints of lamb with a mountain of vegetables and potatoes as well as an enormous mound of the ubiquitous pasta being rolled and cut into shape.

They had risen early that morning and the family had gone to mass before they followed the traditional Easter procession around the village, bearing the statue of the Madonna and the holy relics from the church. Giulia had told her that one year in a nearby town she had been to see the penitents in their white hooded robes and bare feet, carrying candles in the gloom. "It was quite eerie," she said.

Sam saw there was a curious white grain grown entirely in the dark arranged around the sepulchre and for lunch they had a kind of sour pizza with onions and sultanas as a form of penance. That was of course before the boys indulged in even more chocolate.

"A long time ago before we had our own oven all the bread and pizzas were cooked by the baker in a communal oven," Maria explained. "We would make the dough at home and take it there. Meat as well, though that was scarce then." She showed Sam the little wooden carving with the imprint of their initials on the bottom, used to press into the dough before it was cooked to tell the baker which loaf was which.

They had also paid a visit to the little churchyard to honour the ancestors, including Maria's father and mother, her grandparents and both of Enrico's parents and grandparents.

Sam remembered coming here after Federico's abrupt departure at Ferragusto to recover herself in this peaceful spot with pictures of the dead on the tombs amid the dark cypress trees, the spring sunshine gleaming on the white marble. Sam could think of worse places to be buried.

They spent a lazy hour after lunch looking through the family photo album with Giulia pointing out relatives who had immigrated to America when times had been hard, with some of whom, sadly, they had lost touch.

"Every so often though," Giulia said, "we get an unexpected phone call from someone who wants to trace their roots and who turns out to be a distant cousin, which is very exciting. A few years ago we discovered we had a big group of relations living in Brazil."

Then Sam came across a tiny snap of a small child aged about two dressed in the garb of a Pierrot.

"Who's that?" She asked curiously.

Giulia leant over and scrutinised the print. "Oh, it's Federico," she laughed. "Doesn't he look cute?"

"Yes, he does," Sam replied, "very cute," thinking that that was what his children would look like. She kept her head bowed so that Giulia wouldn't see her expression.

On Easter Sunday, they watched the Pope's broadcast from St Peter's Square in Rome. The family had gone to church in the early morning and come back with palm crosses.

"Monday though," Giulia explained, "Monday is a happy day. We call it Pasquetta, a sort of little Easter where we bless hardboiled eggs and have fun."

They perambulated around the village greeting everyone and wishing Happy Easter to all the friends and relatives. Sam and Giulia smiled at the sight of Giulia's brother Giovanni covertly holding hands with the girl they had seen him chatting to at the Sagra. They ducked away before Giovanni turned round and spotted them and was embarrassed.

Then it was time to go back down to Naples and the uncles and prepare for a busy summer season. Sam was full of fresh ideas for painting, some of which she thought might include blessing painted hard boiled eggs! There was never a lack of inspiration for her work.

Chapter 27

Just before Easter, it had been Uncle Richard Saint's day.

Sam had soon learnt that in Italy the day of the Saint after whom you were named was a cause for celebration. Even more important than your birthday in fact. Gianfranco, treating them to arias from the Barber of Seville which they were due to see at the opera house that night, had been cooking all morning. Because it was his special day Richard was allowed a reprieve from the strict diet Gianfranco had put him on. His eyes lit up at the sight of the steaming mound of ravioli laid in front of him. He ate voraciously like a starving prisoner at last released from custody. His solitary glass of red wine, because Gianfranco was still being strict about that, was soon downed and he fingered his glass impatiently, looking hopefully at the bottle, but Gianfranco ignored the glances even though Richard said pointedly that he'd read somewhere that red wine was full of iron and very good for you. Even when Gianfranco left the room to fetch another plate he gave strict instructions to Sam not to allow Richard another glass. She in turn and in solidarity only drank one glass.

The meal had been interrupted constantly by telephone calls wishing Richard 'Auguri', best wishes, for his Onomastico, his Saint's day. Richard had beamed with pleasure at each call, receiving every message with the dignity it deserved as if he were royalty, or at least king for the day.

Gianfranco appeared with a huge roast chicken cooked with rosemary surrounded by potatoes and a side salad. When they had finished eating Richard leant back with a satisfied staff sigh, loosening his trouser belt a couple of notches.

"First proper meal I've had in months," he said with a mixture of reproach and gratitude.

"Well, you know it's for your own good," Gianfranco had replied, kissing the top of Richard's bald head. "We want to have you around for a little longer don't we Sam?"

Sam agreed with a smile. She loved to see the affection between the two of them. True love was love in whatever form it took, she mused.

Thinking of love made her wistful. She wasn't in the least bit jealous of Giulia and Alberto; she was of course, delighted for them, but she knew she was still longing for the love of an unattainable man who had, it seemed, just been flirting with her and despite his protestations, leading her on while being attached to someone else all along. He obviously wasn't worth worrying about if he was that sort of person. She must shut him out of her mind and her heart, but it was so difficult, so very difficult not to remember the feeling of his lips on hers, how they had danced closely together in the village square, his breath on her cheek, his eyes gazing into hers.

"You are looking serious carissima," Richard said stroking her cheek. "What is it? Still thinking about that handsome young doctor?"

She flushed. "No, no," she lied. "I was just thinking how lucky I was to be here. You are both so kind to me. I am so grateful to you for putting up with me."

They both looked at her in astonishment.

"Putting up with you?" Richard said. "Not in the slightest! What makes you think that? You are our greatest asset. What would we have done without you, especially after our fraught few months when I was ill. You held things together wonderfully, working all hours without complaining, not to mention all those fantastic pictures which have everybody flocking to buy them. No, no it it us who should be thanking you."

"Absolutamente, absolutely. You are favalosa," agreed Gianfranco.

Sam's lips were trembling. "Oh, thank you." was all she could say. She felt so emotional at their kind words and the only thing she could do was hug them both. "Thank you. Thank you so much."

Gianfranco then went to fetch the special dessert he had made for his Ricardo, a tiramisu which he knew was Richard's favourite. Richard was almost overwhelmed at being allowed to have so many calories after months of deprivation.

"You know what it means?" He said to Sam as he helped himself to an extra-large spoonful, then, defiantly, another large spoonful, with Gianfranco shrugging in resignation.

"Something about picking you up?" Suggested Sam, helping herself to the rich concoction of chocolate cream and amaretti biscuits drenched in marsala wine.

"Exactly that," Richard said, "well, it certainly cheered me up!"

"Not sure about being picked up," Sam laughed. "I don't think anyone could pick me up after that huge meal. Thank you Gianfranco. That was delicious."

After their coffee, Sam left the two of them for their siesta and went downstairs to the gallery to check a few things. She loved wandering around the light and airy space, especially now that it held quite a few of her own pictures. She couldn't help but be proud. At first, she thought the uncles were just indulging her, but now as they were "selling like hot panini," she smiled, she was delighted to find she could now truly call herself a successful artist.

They sold an eclectic mix: a few prints of old masters, especially those to be found in Naples like the Caravaggios, and prints of modern artists like Warhol or Banksy's Madonna, and Picasso and Dali prints also sold well; then many originals done by local artists in oil and watercolour. Also quirky things like cartoons of Maradona, who had played for Naples. His portrait was also all over the city painted on the side of apartment blocks. He was worshipped like a god.

She came to the section of her own paintings and found there were two more with red dots signifying that they had been sold, but not yet collected. That must have been recent as she hadn't noticed. Out of curiosity, she looked up the buyer in the large accounts ledger and gasped in astonishment. There on the page in black and white was his name.

Federico.

It was Federico who had bought the paintings. He must have come in when she was out on an errand. She hadn't seen him since that occasion in the market at Christmas time with her parents and had long ago given up hope that he would give Nadia up and choose her.

She found herself crying with a mixture of joy, rage and frustration. She had vowed to wipe him out of her life and her heart but now she once again felt a surge of hope.

Why would he buy her pictures if she didn't mean anything to him? What on earth was going on?

Chapter 28

Not only had he bought her pictures, but several weeks after that Giulia told her something that made her heart leap with hope once again.

They were sitting at lunch in Maria's busy kitchen, finishing yet another delicious meal, when Giulia looked at her father and said, "Papa, wasn't there something you were going to ask Sam?"

He looked at her gravely, "Yes," he said, stroking his chin, "now I wonder what it was?" He frowned.

Sam looked from one smiling face to the other.

"Stop teasing her, Papa," Giulia laughed. The family were looking on in anticipation and the boys were giggling.

"Well," Enrico said slowly, "we were thinking," he paused for dramatic effect "the village council and I that is…" He paused again.

"Oh, stop it, Papa, and let the poor girl out of her misery."

"Well the fact is." There was a metaphorical roll of drums, "We would like to have an exhibition of your work here in the village."

Sam gazed at him, open-mouthed with surprise. "Well, I," she stammered. "But have you asked the uncles?"

"Absolutely and they are perfectly in agreement. After all, most of your paintings are set here and the majority of the villagers haven't had a chance to see them. I know you've shown them to the individuals you've painted when you asked their permission, but I'm sure everyone will be delighted to see some more of your work."

"I don't know what to say," Sam stuttered again.

"Why not just say yes?" Giulia touched her arm.

"I should be honoured." Sam conceded.

"And we are honoured to have a famous artist in our midst."

"Are you going to put a plaque up outside the house with her name on it?" Giovanni grinned.

"It might come to that," Giulia said, "and if Sam becomes really famous, you will have to pay to speak to her."

"I don't think that will ever happen," Sam laughed, but she choked with pride at the thought they had asked her and that her pictures were going to be exhibited in the village she loved so much.

So, it was all arranged. Forty of her pictures and several dozen prints were carefully packaged and driven up in the gallery van by Gianfranco.

The council room in the village square had been cleared and the furniture stored for the two week duration of the exhibition.

Sam decided on the arrangement of the pictures and a poster had been printed as well as flyers for the surrounding villages and towns. They spent the day hanging the pictures, deterring a few of the villagers who were desperately trying to peek through the windows.

The queue on the first day was so long they had to ration the number of people allowed in at any one time. Everyone had wanted to be the first on this important day.

Those that came in at the head, some of whom didn't realise that 'the English girl' was an artist, exclaimed in wonder when they saw their fellow villagers depicted in paint.

"But that's old Francesco from the cobbler's shop!" they exclaimed, or "Look, look, it's Gianetta from the baker's." They argued about which balcony you could see the view of the river from and who it was sitting at the cafe in the square. There were, of course, many 'suggestive angles', little picturesque squares and flights of steps and there were squeals of delight when their own particular square was recognised or that of one of their relatives.

Sam stood by smiling in gratitude as the praise flowed.

There were a handful of tourists still around and some were bought by them but many of the villagers wanted a picture too. Even some people from the surrounding villages asked if she would come and paint there. She said she would be delighted and gave them her phone number so they could make arrangements for a day when she could go and make preliminary sketches.

She had previously completed the picture of Alfredo and his baby brother as a christening present but when Alfredo came with his parents to the exhibition he tugged at his father's sleeve, begging for him to buy the one of the children playing outside the school house. Which he did with pleasure.

She did give, as a present, a sketch she had done of the old lady with the donkey carrying the wood, as a thank you for that day when she helped to clear up the smashed melon and the old lady was delighted.

She also thrilled Giulia by saying that she wanted a share of her profit to go towards the school.

"Thank you so much, Sam," Giulia hugged her. "That is so kind of you. I know exactly what I shall use it for. I want to buy some proper shelves for our little library. Many of the books have been stored in boxes for ages because I had nowhere to put them."

Enrico also bought one of her special pictures, a large depiction of the villagers taking their evening walk, the passeggiata, in the village square, as a permanent fixture for the council offices.

At the end of the two weeks, the exhibition was over and the unsold paintings had to be returned to the gallery in Naples, but in fact there were very few left because they had proved so popular.

"It will be nice for your father to have his council office back," Sam said to Giulia as they packed the pictures away.

"Yes, but it has been such fun, hasn't it?" Giulia said. "And so good for everyone to see themselves. The villagers that haven't been painted are quite jealous. To be immortalised in paint by our 'local' artist was quite a feather in some people's caps I think."

"Oh dear," Sam said, "I shall have to paint more pictures and try and include more people."

"No peace for the wicked," Giulia laughed.

"Seriously though," Sam said. "Thank you so much Giulia for suggesting the exhibition. It was such a pleasure to have my paintings here in the village."

"Oh, it wasn't me who suggested it," Giulia said, looking at her friend "It was Federico."

Sam went very quiet. "I see," she said eventually, "that was very good of him."

"I think," Giulia said slowly, "that you are very important to him. I've seen the way he looks at you and I know he comes here especially to meet you. I'm not sure what is happening between you, but don't give up yet."

With that, Sam began to cry and once she started the floodgates opened and she couldn't stop. All the pent-up feelings she had been holding back for so long were suddenly released and she clung to her friend, sobbing on her shoulder, telling her everything that had been happening between herself and Federico. Giulia held her, shocked at the depth of Sam's emotion and also at the way Federico had been behaving, but, having no words of comfort to give her, could only stroke her hair soothingly until the tears ceased.

Chapter 29

It was to be Maria's 50th birthday on the following Sunday and Enrico had arranged to take her out to dinner at an exclusive restaurant in the nearby town.

If Maria was disappointed that they hadn't arranged a party for her she was far too modest to say so. She did however buy a new dress for herself in anticipation of her birthday dinner.

On the Friday before the big day, Enrico told her that one of his fellow mayors, someone from a town near Naples, was having a reception, a special party to celebrate the town's 'twinning' with another town in southern France and he and Maria were invited. She was pleased that at least the new dress would have at least more than one airing and was dressed and ready by 6. 30 on the evening in question. The boys both gave a wolf whistle as she appeared in her finery with her hair newly coiled in a fashionable chignon and she thanked them graciously. They had told her they were due to play in a football match against the next village that evening and Maria said how sorry she was that she was unable to be there to support them.

"Don't worry, Mum, it's just a friendly," they assured her.

Giulia and Sam too complimented her on her appearance and told her they were going to spend the evening planning the next school outing together.

Once Maria and Enrico had left the house, the four of them raced to get changed, ran down the hill, leapt into Giulia's car and set off for Naples.

If Maria wondered why they were going on a roundabout route to the town in question it didn't occur to her to ask Enrico what was going on until they entered the outskirts of Naples and she suddenly found herself outside Richard and Gianfranco's art gallery.

"Just popping in to say hello to Richard and Gianfranco before we move on," said Enrico cheerfully, holding the car door open for her and helping her out of the passenger seat.

As they entered the art gallery it was in total darkness.

Then suddenly all the lights came on and it took Maria a moment to realise that inside the gallery was a vast crowd of people, all staring at her and yelling, "Sorpresa! Surprise!"

She burst into tears.

And surprise it was indeed to see Giulia, Sam and the boys all dressed up when she had left them in the village less than two hours before, not to mention Richard, Gianfranco, Enrico's sister and her family and a whole host of other friends and relations all smiling and shouting, "Auguri, best wishes. Buon Compleanno, happy birthday."

The uncles and Sam had arranged a laden buffet table and a bar overflowing with wine and Prosecco which was enthusiastically being poured by Giovanni and Tommaso and, after the initial shock, Maria was soon loving being the centre of attention. She was showered with flowers, boxes of chocolates and pieces of jewellery and was extremely touched when Sam gave her a very special picture she had painted of herself, Enrico, Giulia and the boys sitting on the balcony of their home with a view of the mountains behind them.

Then she was given an envelope by Enrico and the children, with contributions, Sam noticed, not only from Richard and Gianfranco but also from Federico, was a voucher for a week's holiday with Enrico in a luxury hotel on the Isle of Capri, a place that Maria had long expressed a desire to visit. She had in fact never managed to travel much so this to her was a really exotic trip. She was thrilled.

Sam, laughing at the expression of pleasure on her face, found herself looking straight into Federico's eyes as he stood behind Maria. He gazed back at her and smiled. She smiled back, then immediately averted her eyes, unable to bear the sudden shaft of pain she felt. She had spent weeks trying to forget him and had told herself firmly that she must move on.

Sadly, it was all in vain as all the old emotions came flooding back at the sight of him.

She kept herself busy by picking up a bottle and circling the room with it, topping up glasses, determined to avoid him.

In the meantime, she heard Maria, despite her pleasure at the thought of a holiday spent being pampered and away from housework and cooking for a week, saying anxiously that the family would never be able to cope without her.

"Well," Giulia answered with a smile. "It's true I will be busy with the school and unable to help much but the boys will have to step up and show how much they have learnt from the cookery lessons you have given them, won't they? And I am sure they will be very good too at shopping for food, making beds, sweeping the floor, doing the washing and ironing, tending to the garden and all the other million and one things you do by yourself without complaining won't they?"

The boys looked suitably crest-fallen and Maria didn't appear totally reassured, but everyone laughed.

An enormous birthday cake was wheeled in on a trolley, Maria blew out the candles and everyone sang lustily "Buon Compleanno, happy birthday to you," with descants from the choir of the church of San Nicola at the top of the hill in the village and Maria was once again overwhelmed with emotion. "Brindisi," they all shouted. "A toast to the birthday girl," and they all raised their glasses and cheered.

Gianfranco slapped Richard's hand as he reached for a third slice of cake.

"Thank you, thank you all," Maria said. "I had no idea. You kept the secret well." And, she added, "I will have several more chances to wear my new dress if I'm going to a luxury hotel. Also," looking at Enrico, "perhaps I will also need a new handbag and a new pair of shoes to go with it."

Chapter 30

Sam was sitting on Giulia's balcony sketching the distant view. The family were out and she was taking advantage of the quiet time.

She was concentrating so hard that she was shocked when a voice behind her said, "That's wonderful. You really are very talented."

She looked up and felt the colour drain from her face.

Federico!

He was standing gazing down at her.

She got up hurriedly, knocking the chair over as she did so. He bent and righted it. They were close together, very close. She felt herself trembling.

He leant forward and kissed her. Her eyes closed and a thrill went through her as she savoured the feeling of his lips on hers. Then she drew back.

"No," she said. "No please, not again."

"I am sorry," he said. "You are right. This is not right. I must speak to Nadia but it has been difficult. Her father has been ill."

Was this yet another excuse? she thought. Or was it genuine? How was she to know the truth?

She gazed at him, the longing in her eyes was obvious to him but so too was the longing in his eyes obvious to her too.

Then they were kissing again, frantically.

At last, he stepped back. "I have been yearning to do that," he said, "lying awake at night thinking of you, desperate to see you, but I understand I have not behaved well. You must think I am not an honourable person."

She was silent and he flushed, knowing that that was how she felt.

"I didn't want to be in this position, but I am, and I know I must sort it out."

"Yes, you must."

They were still close together and she found herself moving towards him. Then they were kissing frantically again. She was shaking with emotion. Then she drew back in alarm. It wasn't emotion she was shaking with. The whole room was rocking.

"What is it? What is happening?" She gasped. She was aware of the light bulb swinging on the ceiling and there was a loud rumbling sound.

"Terremoto. It's an earthquake. Quick, under the table," he said urgently. He pulled her down and beneath the table, his arm around her to try and protect her. The room was swaying and the china on the shelves began to drop and crash to the floor. The photos and pictures were falling off the walls. Sam felt as if she was on board a ship in a rough sea.

It seemed like an eternity before the rumbling and crashing stopped but it was perhaps only a few minutes before the room was still again.

"Are you ok?" He whispered. His face was close to hers as they lay entwined under the table.

They crawled out together and as they did so a plate which had been teetering on the edge of the dresser fell and hit her on the head. There was a sudden darkness as she lost consciousness.

**

She came too with Federico's anxious face hovering over her.

"Sam, carissima, my darling."

"What happened?" She muttered.

"A plate, it fell and knocked you out. My god. For a moment I thought I'd lost you." He held her tightly, forgetting for a moment all his medical training in the panic of the moment. Although her head hurt she relished the look on his face and the feeling of him being close to her.

"You must lie still," he said. "You may have a concussion." He was crouched on the floor beside her, holding her in his arms. After a while, her head cleared and she felt much better, but she wanted to make the most of this sensation of his arms around her and the surge of joy she felt that it was obvious that he did care for her deeply.

"I think I am alright now," she whispered at last.

"OK, but you must be careful. Don't move too suddenly."

"No, no. I'll be fine. We must see what has happened outside. Giulia, the family. We must find them. People may be hurt. They will need you."

She rose shakily to her feet and, leaning on him, they moved together towards the door.

"Watch out," he said, "there may be aftershocks. Some of the buildings may not be safe."

They crept out of the house after struggling with the door which had become distorted on its hinges.

There was an eerie quietness in the street as they stood outside. There were bricks and roof tiles, overturned pots of flowers with the earth scattered everywhere. They picked their way carefully towards the village square. Then they began to hear shouting and screaming.

As they entered the square they saw Giulia's anxious face.

"Oh Sam, Federico, thank God you are alright."

She didn't seem to wonder about them being together.

"We were in the house," Sam said. "It is a mess, but alright. Your family, are they all ok?"

"Yes, yes, Mamma and Babbo, my dad are here helping. The boys too. But there are people hurt. Federico, we need you."

"Show me where," he said. Then he added "Look after Sam. She got knocked out. I think she is ok but she may have a concussion."

"No, I must help," Sam said. She followed after Federico and Giulia.

It suddenly occurred to her that the epicentre of the earthquake wasn't in the village. Where was the centre? Was it in Naples? She panicked about the uncles. Were they hurt? With trembling hands she pulled out her phone and punched in the number of the gallery.

The line was dead. There was no signal.

She must also find a way of telling her parents back in England that she was alright. If it was a big earthquake it would be on the news and they would be worried. There was nothing she could do until she got a signal.

She was close to a small knot of people in the corner of the square where Federico was already hard at work assessing a few of the figures. Mostly it was all bumps and bruises, but a child with an obviously broken arm was crying and she watched as Federico tenderly and competently found something to use as a temporary splint and bound it up. His soothing words to her calmed her and she soon stopped crying.

There was the sound of sirens in the distance and blue lights flashed along the mountain roads. She watched as the lights came nearer, then abruptly stopped about a mile away.

"Must be a landslide," Giulia said, "or a falling wall. Maybe the road is blocked." There was the distant sound of shouting echoing across the valley as people were trying to remove the blockage.

The men of the village had been scouting around, checking all the houses to see if there was anyone trapped and to see how bad the damage was, but it seemed that there was relatively little damage and as far as they knew everyone was accounted for. There was something to be said, Sam thought, for living in a village, a close community where everyone knew everyone else and they looked after each other.

The shouting on the hillside intensified and eventually the sound of the sirens started up again as the blockage was cleared.

Federico was still attending to cuts and bruises but, aside from the girl with the broken arm, there were no other injuries.

An ambulance appeared at last and the girl, together with her anxious mother, was taken away to have her arm properly set.

"I have to get back to Naples," Federico said. "I don't know how bad things are there. Even if the epicentre wasn't in Naples itself they may be bringing casualties in from the villages."

"Will you take me?" Sam asked. "I have to see if the uncles are alright."

"Of course."

So, leaving Giulia and her mother to deliver sugared drinks for shock and generally tend to the villagers and help clear up the mess, they prepared to leave.

Already the square was buzzing with the excited chatter that came after the relief that everyone was safe and Sam bade farewell to Giulia and her family and climbed into Federico's car.

"I pray that there are no aftershocks," he said.

The road was long and winding. He drove as fast as he dared, skilfully avoiding the blockages because the road was littered with fallen branches and broken walls.

Sam sat in silence, still shocked by the experience she had gone through and what seemed like a very lucky escape.

Federico too was silent as he concentrated on the road. There was a grim expression on his face and all traces of the intimate moments they had shared had vanished, as if they had never been.

Finally, though Sam plucked up the courage to ask, "Tell me, why did you come to the village today?"

He didn't hesitate but replied immediately. "Because I hoped you would be there. I was desperate to see you again."

"I'm glad," Sam replied.

There was nothing more to be said really and, despite a head that was beginning to ache from the blow she had received, she was overwhelmed with happiness once more.

They left the mountain road at last and took the autostrada to Naples. They gazed around them as they drove they realised with a sigh of relief that there was no damage.

They arrived at last. It seemed that the epicentre of the earthquake had not been Naples at all. It was in its usual chaotic state as they drove through the crowded streets, but the earthquake had been a minor one and only affected a few small villages on the outskirts.

"Thank you," she said as they reached the door of the gallery.

He leant over and kissed her. "I will sort it out. I really will," he promised. "Sorry, I must go. Maybe I won't contact you again until I have told her. It wouldn't be fair."

"Alright," she said. This time it had to be true. It had to be.

She watched after his departing car then opened the door and went inside.

The uncles looked up in surprise. "Oh, Sam, you are back early. We didn't expect you until tomorrow."

Sam immediately burst into tears as all the emotions of the day crowded in on her at once.

"My dear girl, whatever is it? What has happened?"

It was obvious that they hadn't realised what had occurred, had heard nothing about any earthquake and their faces were pictures of concern as she told them about the events of the day.

"I couldn't phone you because there was no signal." She sobbed as she sat on the sofa with an uncle on each side, each with a comforting arm around her.

They fussed over her, bringing her drinks for shock. "But how did you get back?" Richard asked.

Sam explained.

"Ah, the handsome doctor," Richard said. "Are things better in that department?"

"Maybe," Sam admitted and he gave her arm a comforting squeeze.

She phoned her parents, then wished she hadn't because as earthquakes go it was only a mild one, not even making the national news and now they would only worry. She supposed it was selfish really. She had just wanted to hear the sound of her parents' voices.

***

The following week was a busy one. Sam phoned Giulia. There had been no more tremors and it seemed the region had got away really lightly, but the after-effects lingered for Sam as every time a coach rumbled past the gallery or a gust of wind blew a curtain noisily across, she imagined the tremors all over again.

She didn't hear from Federico. She didn't expect to, but she prayed that he hadn't changed his mind again, that he regretted promising her that he would speak to Nadia.

The memory of his lips on hers was tangible. She would put her fingers up and touch her mouth as if she could recreate that intense feeling again. She could still remember the look on his face when she had come around after being knocked out, that expression of passionate love and concern. Surely he meant it this time. He really would speak to Nadia.

Surely he would.

She didn't visit the village for weeks, partly because the gallery was busy but partly because she felt she must leave Giulia and her family to clear up the mess wrought by the tremors and the last thing they needed was a visitor. She rang Giulia often though to see how things were going. She asked if the school was damaged and was glad to find out that it was completely unscathed, so lessons had resumed. She also asked after the little girl with a broken arm and was relieved to find that she was enjoying her new-found celebrity with her friends queuing up to write messages on the plaster and to have the honour of being the only person to be injured during the terrible earthquake that had devastated the village and that she had been lucky to survive. Her words, of course.

In the meantime, Sam waited impatiently for a call, but the weeks passed and it did not come.

Chapter 31

Giulia and Alberto weren't having a traditional hen and stag party. They had invited all their friends for a trip on the sea for the day.

Despite living near the bay of Naples, Sam had rarely had the chance to go out in a boat so she was looking forward to it. It promised to be fun.

They all drove in hired cars with drivers (drinking was expected!) to the nearest point on the coast where it had been arranged for several speedboats to pick them up. They divided into two groups with Giulia in one with the girls and the other with Alberto and the boys.

Including Federico.

True to his word he hadn't contacted her. She still didn't know if he had spoken to Nadia.

It was going to be a difficult day after all and she must make sure she had as little contact with him as possible. She could remain polite and distant in front of her friends and there were plenty of people to talk to without it seeming odd that they weren't communicating.

The engines revved.

"Avanti Ragazzi! Let's go everyone!" Shouted Giulia and Alberto in unison. With a roar they were off, crashing across the waves and hitting the crest of each one with a tremendous thud.

No one had been told where they were going but when they finally dropped anchor it was in a tiny cove of stunning turquoise water with a fine white crescent of sand.

After the roar of the engines ceased silence descended for a long moment.

There were twenty of them altogether, ten in each boat. Sam had watched the boats being loaded with bags of fruit and bread, not to mention several large crates of wine.

The first thing though was that it was all overboard for a swim to the grotto. The whole group dived in one after the other, including Sam.

"You can swim?" Giulia had asked anxiously. "I never thought to ask."

Sam smiled "School champion," she said modestly. "I swam for the county."

Giulia laughed, "I should have known. You are, as I think you say, a dark horse. You are so talented in so many ways but you never say anything."

The sea at the entrance to the grotto was a wonderful emerald green and they plunged under the water to admire the magnificent stalactites and stalagmites in the eerie light and suddenly a hand touched her arm. She turned her head.

Federico was swimming alongside her.

She swam to the surface. She could just about see his face in the dimness of the cave.

"You are not speaking to me?"

"No, no, I mean yes," Sam spluttered, momentarily taken off guard.

"You are a good swimmer."

"Thank you."

They lapsed into an awkward silence once more. She was desperate to know if he had spoken to Nadia, if there was any hope at all, but it was not the time or the place to speak of such things, surrounded as they were by happy, joking people.

Eventually, they turned and swam back to the boats, everyone hauling themselves aboard, dripping and laughing. There was no need even for towels as the sun was hot now and they dried quickly, the rays beating down on their heads fiercely and glinting like a treasure trove of golden coins on the water.

She closed her eyes and savoured the sun on her face the inside of her eyelids burning red.

She heard the pop of a cork and then another and the sound of wine being poured into beakers. Someone thrust one into her hand and she sipped the cool white wine and thought nothing could be better than sitting here in this paradise. It only needed one other thing to make her life complete and it seemed that would never happen.

Her thoughts drifted to what they were going to have for lunch. The swim had made her hungry. Ham? Cheese? Carciofi? those lovely pickled artichokes the Italians do so well? She hadn't noticed any of that being loaded onto the boats.

Then Giulia tapped her on the shoulder. "Come on, let's go…"

"Go? Go where?"

"Lunch." Giulia grinned. "You are going to have to work for it."

Sam was bewildered.

Giulia took pity on her, "Frutta Di Mare. We are going to catch our own lunch from the sea." She handed Sam a pair of flippers, a snorkel and a knife, together with a thick pair of gloves.

They slid over the side.

"Ricci. Look down there."

She pointed down through the clear blue water. "Sea urchins," she explained, "those black waving spines."

Sam was puzzled "But how are we going to cook them?"

"Cook them? No, we eat them raw. We need the females, those with eggs."

"How can I tell the difference?"

"I will show you. They are paler in colour than the males, but," she continued, "please be very careful not to tread on one. If you get a spine in your foot it is very, very painful and you could even end up in hospital."

"Ok, I'll try very hard not to do that."

They snorkelled along and Giulia, wearing thick gloves, carefully prized the urchins off the rocks, handing them to Sam to put in a bag. When it was full they surfaced and tossed the bag over the side of the boat.

Alberto in the meanwhile was also busy with a knife, prizing limpets off the rocks. "Patelli," he explained. Sam could see how they got their reputation for clinging. It was hard work.

"Polpo," someone shouted. It was a small octopus which they held up, its tentacles dangling. They threw it back in, much to her relief; then a family of crabs.

"Attento!" someone shouted. "Meduse."

Away to Sam's right she could see a host of ghostly shapes drifting through the water, their tentacles waving gently. Jellyfish!

They all moved swiftly away and climbed back into the boats until the jellyfish had moved away to a safe distance.

"They weren't the really deadly ones like those you get in the Pacific which can kill you, but they still give you a nasty sting," Giulia said.

Someone had caught mussels and everyone set to opening the catch. The sea urchins were cut open with what looked like huge shears to reveal the bright orange eggs, arranged inside in a beautiful petal shape.

More wine was poured, crisp rolls were produced and fresh lemons, picked that morning from the tree in Giulia's garden and still with the leaves on them, and fat juicy tomatoes, also from the garden.

The seafood was occasionally rubbery and sometimes gritty, but Sam tasted the full flavour of the sea. With the sun and the wine, it had to be almost the most memorable meal she had ever had, not counting the one with Federico in his father's house.

To follow there were ripe peaches and apricots, the juice running down their chins.

A large melon was produced, but the knife to cut it was in the other boat. Sam volunteered to swim over and fetch it.

She slipped over the side and as she hit the water she wondered for a moment if she was doing the right thing. The sun and the wine had done strange things to her vision.

She hauled herself up onto the other boat, very aware that it was Federico who was offering a helping hand.

"Grazie," she muttered, trying to avoid looking into his eyes. She chatted a while with Alberto and the other friends until there was a call from the first boat complaining that she hadn't brought the knife back. So, putting the knife between her teeth, pirate fashion, she once again slipped over the side and swam back.

She wasn't exactly sure how it happened or why she put her foot down: but put it down she did.

She yelped, the knife falling out of her mouth.

It was like a bee or a wasp sting, only far, far worse.

She gasped in pain "My foot, my foot is hurting. Ow!" She cried.

"Oh, no," Giulia said. "It could be a sea urchin."

The occupants of the second boat had heard the commotion. Sam was aware of a splash and in a few moments, Federico was at her side. Holding her arm he swam with her to the beach. With his help, she hopped out of the water and collapsed onto the sand. She felt tears springing into her eyes, the pain was so bad.

Federico helped her onto a convenient rock. "Let me look," he said gently.

He took her foot very carefully in his hands.

"Ah," he said, "as I thought, a richio, a sea urchin spine."

"Giulia warned me but I never thought…Can you get it out?" She winced.

"Of course, I'm a doctor, aren't I?" He smiled reassuringly.

"Yes, yes, of but please hurry, it hurts so much. Can't you just pull it out?"

"No, I can't. If I leave some part of the spine in, it will become infected."

"So what will you do?"

"Acete. Vinegar."

By this time, a concerned group had gathered around them.

"Giulia, could you please get some vinegar?"

"Of course."

She sprinted across the sand and swam back to the boat where luckily they had brought some vinegar for the salad.

"What does the vinegar do?" Sam asked.

"Dissolves it."

Someone from the back of the group made a remark that she didn't quite catch and there was a ripple of laughter.

"Not funny," Federico said, "and not true."

"What did he say?" Sam asked. "I didn't catch that."

"A suggestion. How do you say it in English? An old wives tale? If you use urine," he met her gaze. "Don't worry, I won't use that."

Despite her agony, she smiled. "Thank you," she said, "but to be honest I don't care what you try as long as you stop the pain."

Giulia had arrived back with the vinegar and, kneeling at her feet and working very carefully, he poured some on the sole of her foot. She watched as the spine began to dissolve and he slowly pulled it out.

"Better?" He asked, looking up at her.

"Yes, much," she said. "Thank heavens you were here." She managed another smile "Or someone might have used…"

"Urine?" He grinned, then he said, "Can you walk?"

He helped her to her feet and she, leaning against him, hobbled along. The pain was beginning to subside but she suppressed a wicked thought. She was going to make the most of being close to him and being held tight even if it was futile.

She stumbled.

"Here," he said "I will carry you to the car so you can rest."

Giulia and Alberto, aware that they would all be drinking had arranged for the cars to pick them up at the end of the day but someone had phoned to ask a car to come early to take her back to the village.

Giulia was there as the car drew up, waiting anxiously "I'll go with her," she said.

"No," Sam protested, "it's your party. I already feel bad enough, spoiling your day. I'll be fine."

"But," Giulia protested, but Federico cut across her protest and said firmly, "I'm the doctor here. I'll go back with her, make sure she's alright. I need to look after my patient and ensure there is no allergic reaction."

So, Giulia reluctantly agreed. She brought them their clothes so they could cover up and watched as Federico helped Sam into the car and settled himself in beside her.

Sam gave a rueful half wave as the car moved away and the driver began the trip round the mountain roads.

"I am glad we have this chance to talk." Federico said. "I wanted to see you alone, but it has been difficult."

Then he glanced at the driver. "Maybe not now."

They sat in silence as the car sped along but he was holding her hand and it was a companionable silence, not fraught with tension as their other meetings had been.

They arrived back in the village and he carried her up the hill to the house.

"Sorry," she said. "I shouldn't have had so much lunch."

"To be honest, I'm rather enjoying it." He was surprisingly strong.

They were passing curious villagers, each one asking what was wrong, but as soon as he said "Sea Urchin," they nodded in concern.

They arrived at the house at last and Maria answered his knock.

Federico explained.

"Oh cara. How sad for you. Is it very sore?"

"Much better now," Sam said, "thanks to Federico. It's a good thing he was there or I might have part of the spine still in my foot."

He carried her into the bedroom and Maria brought in a basin of hot water and a towel.

Then she glanced at the pair of them. Maria was not a stupid woman and she knew it was time to withdraw and leave them alone. She had long noticed something between them but had stayed silent, hoping that she was correct.

She smiled to herself and as she settled herself on the balcony with a basket of broad beans waiting to be podded she hummed happily.

"That's Amore," seemed the most appropriate tune in the circumstances.

Chapter 32

In the bedroom, Federico carefully bathed her foot. Sam felt tingles up her spine at the touch of his hands. There was something particularly erotic about the way he was stroking it.

"You were going to talk to me," she encouraged him.

His head was still bent over her foot and he didn't raise it. There was a pause. She held her breath. Finally, he began.

"I have told you about the situation with Nadia," he said "and that I might have gone on to marry her, if I hadn't met you and realised what real love was."

Sam waited, her heart pounding.

"It has been hard but I finally understood how wrong it would have been to marry someone just because you were friends and liked them. I was desperate though not to hurt her feelings, caught in a trap if you like."

Sam's mind flashed back to how she had felt about Alberto and she had some sympathy for him.

"I was going to speak to her weeks ago, but as I told you her father was ill. He is now much better thank heavens, but there never seemed to be the right moment."

Sam waited. "Then last week," he continued, "we were out walking and she stopped suddenly, turned to me and said.

'That English girl at the gallery, you really like her, don't you? She could see by my face what I felt for you.' Ah, she said, 'I knew I was right.'"

"I said I was sorry, that I loved her as a friend and always would, but if there had ever been an understanding between our families that we would marry, that was now impossible."

He stopped again.

"She turned to look at me and then she surprised me. She smiled. She told me that at first, she was very hurt, but then she began to realise that she felt the same way about me as I did about her: that we were very dear friends, but nothing more. In fact, she said it was watching me looking at you that made her realise what true passion was and that she didn't feel the same way about me either and hoped that someday she would meet someone she could share that feeling with."

He looked up at Sam and there were tears in his eyes. "I am so sorry I have caused you to doubt me. I had to be sure I was doing the right thing. Sam, I love you and I want to marry you."

Sam felt her heart was going to burst with joy.

Then she started to giggle.

He looked alarmed, "What is it? Don't you want me after all?"

Sam felt hysteria rising in her, "No, it's not that," she gasped, "It's just that I never imagined in my wildest dreams someone proposing to me while he was still holding my foot. Do you think you could let it go for a moment and kiss me?"

He let go immediately and did as she had instructed.

Very hard.

Very hard indeed.

Much later Sam, lying in his arms asked, "When did you first know that you had feelings for me?"

He laughed, "That's easy. It was the moment in the square when this beautiful, screaming woman confronted me with flashing eyes, yelling that I had pushed her over, shouting so loudly that I didn't have time to explain or apologise."

"I think it was the same for me," Sam said. "Even while I was shouting at you, I knew there was something; and when I took your hand after we both apologised it was as if I had known you forever, as if we belonged together."

Much, much later, when they finally emerged from the bedroom, they found the entire family busy with jobs in the kitchen, pretending that they had noticed nothing. Giulia had returned and she took one look at their radiant faces and the fact that they were holding hands and gave Sam a questioning look.

"Everything is alright." Sam said simply. "And I don't mean just with my foot!"

"Wonderful." Giulia said.

And Maria of course said, "supper is ready. A tavola."

They all laughed. Food was the answer to everything.

Chapter 33

Federico gave Sam a small box.

It wasn't hard to guess it was a ring. She hoped desperately that it wasn't a huge, flashy piece of jewellery, but whatever it was she would wear it with pride of course.

She opened the box carefully, holding her breath.

When she saw what was inside she gasped with pleasure. It was an antique ring with a very small, but pretty emerald in the centre, tiny and unostentatious.

"It's perfect," she said, looking up at him in delight.

"Are you sure?" He asked anxiously. "We can buy another ring if you like, something that you choose yourself, but this is my grandmother's engagement ring. My grandparents never had much money, but I know how you feel about showy things and I thought you would like something traditional, something from the village if you like; something that meant a great deal to me as well."

"I am so happy that you thought of something that means so much to both of us and that you understand how I feel about these things."

"Let me put it on," he said.

She held out her hand and he slid the ring onto her finger.

"It fits." She was amazed. "I thought your grandmother would have tiny hands, much smaller than mine."

"Perhaps it's like Cinderella and the glass slipper, with only one person who is the perfect match." He smiled. "My grandmother must have known what was going to happen to her ring after she was gone, that I would choose someone exactly like her in every way."

Then Sam said, "I have something for you in return." She handed him a package.

"What is it?" He asked curiously.

"Well, open it and see."

He unwrapped the parcel carefully.

"Oh, it's one of your paintings," he exclaimed in pleasure.

He looked down at it and was silent for a long while.

"My father's house," he said eventually, his voice husky with emotion.

Then he looked up at her and his eyes were misty. "You couldn't have given me a better present," he said. "When did you paint it?"

"Quite a long time ago, just after the first time you took me there. You remember the day we had lunch together after you helped little Alfredo up the hill?"

"How could I forget it? That was the day I first realised I really was in love with you and knew I had to break up with Nadia somehow."

Then he said, "but you kept it all this time. Why?"

"I don't know. I suppose it was because I wasn't sure how you felt about me. It just never felt the right time."

"Sam, you are a miracle," he said. "Thank you for coming into my life and making me so happy."

"Thank you for coming into mine," she said in return.

***

The first people to tell of course were her parents.

She wondered how her mother was going to take it. Sam understood that she had been hoping that after Sam's 'gap year' as she liked to think of it, she would be coming back to England and settle down to a 'proper job'.

She rang and her mother answered the phone.

"Hi, Mum," Sam said. "I have some news. I'm engaged."

There was silence at the end of the phone and Sam feared the worst. Was her mother going to burst into tears and be upset?

What her mother actually said was "Who to?"

"Federico. You know, you met him that day at the Christmas market. He bought a present for Becka."

"Ah," her mother said, "he was with his lady friend."

"Yes, but that's all sorted. They are just good friends."

"Well thank heavens for that. I had a feeling, the way he looked at you…and the way you looked at him, that something was up. That's wonderful darling, I'm so happy for you."

"Mum," Sam said, "it does mean I'm staying in Italy. I won't be coming home to England to live."

Sam's mother never ceased to surprise her.

"Fantastic news," she said. "You'll be seeing more of us in Italy than you ever would if you were living in a remote part of England. We shall visit so often you'll be sick of seeing us. I'm eager to explore all those places you promised to take us to. In fact, how soon can we come and meet him properly?"

"Whenever you like," Sam laughed.

"And I suppose you'll be getting married in that lovely village?"

"Yes, we'd like to. It means so much to both of us. His father came from there."

Sam could hear sounds "Is that Dad?"

"No, it's Becka. We're looking after her for the weekend."

"Put her on, will you?"

Becka's voice came down the line. "Ciao Sam."

"Ciao, Becka, come stai, how are you?"

"Molto bene, I'm fine. Are you getting married?"

"Yes, I am."

"Goody, I'm going to be a bridesmaid."

Sam laughed that she took it for granted.

"Of course, you are. You are my number one choice."

"Great. Bye, pass you back to granny. I have to feed the cat."

***

Maria too, enveloped her in a warm embrace.

"You have become like a second daughter to me and now we will actually be related. I am so happy for you both. He is a fine young man and you will be good together, very good."

Giulia too, hugged her and said, "Now you really will be like a sister to me and a proper part of the family. We will both be living in Naples so we can see each other all the time."

Sam could see Maria's face at the thought of her daughter leaving home so she said hastily, "But of course, we will be here a lot of the time too. You and Alberto in this house and Federico and I at his father's house."

Even the brothers had soppy grins on their faces.

As for Enrico, well, when he heard the news he burst into tears, tears of joy, of course.

Chapter 34

So, now they were properly engaged.

The uncles were delirious with happiness. They celebrated with a glass, or two in Richard's case, of Prosecco.

"I told you it would work out," Richard said, hugging her. "And even better I hope that means you will stay in Italy now."

Sam replied, laughing, "I suppose so."

There were two things though that were bothering her. One was Nadia; the other, even more important, Federico's mother. The latter they were due to visit the coming weekend and Sam wondered how she would be received: but Nadia was also on her mind.

Had she willingly given Federico up or was she merely saving face, pretending that she didn't care just to make him feel better, when really she cared very deeply? Sam would feel uncomfortable if both or even one of those women resented her. How was she going to get in touch with Nadia though? She couldn't just ring her up. It might look like the victor crowing in triumph at having snatched her boyfriend from under her nose.

The answer came unexpectedly the following Tuesday when the door of the gallery opened and Nadia walked in.

Sam watched in surprise as the elegant figure moved towards her.

"Hello Sam," she said. "I wanted to come and congratulate you. Federico has told me your news."

"Oh, er, thank you," Sam replied. "Actually, I wanted to get in touch. Do you think we could go and get a coffee somewhere?"

"Yes, that would be very nice."

Sam called Gianfranco and asked him to hold the fort for half an hour while she left the gallery.

The two women walked along the Lungomare. They bought a takeaway coffee.

It was difficult for Sam to know how to start the conversation. Eventually she said hesitantly, "Federico told me that you understood about us, that you didn't mind, that you really are happy about the situation. I hope that is true. I would hate to feel that I have snatched him away from you and you are really unhappy, especially as I hope we will be seeing a lot more of each other in the future."

She looked sideways at Nadia's face, trying to gauge her reaction, but for a moment her expression was inscrutable.

Then, to Sam's immense relief, Nadia smiled at her and the smile was genuine. "I have to be frank with you Sam. Federico and I, well he will have told you. We grew up together, shared everything and we sort of drifted along with, I think, both families expecting us to marry. Then, at first, when he met you and I could see he was attracted to you, I was confused. I had to examine my own feelings. I was hurt because I thought he was rejecting me. Then when I really thought about it I realised that the feelings I had for him were more like those of a brother and sister. We are very close, and always will be, so you will have to put up with me being around a lot, but I hope that we will be friends too, you and I. I wanted to make sure that you know that I bear no resentment at all towards you. I am delighted that Federico has found someone he truly loves. I am sure you will make him really happy. Sometimes he can take life a little too seriously and I think you will make him see that life can be fun as well."

She stopped talking. For a moment, Sam couldn't reply; she was overwhelmed with relief and gratitude.

Finally, she said. "Thank you, Nadia. I am so grateful to you for coming and telling me because I didn't want to feel that I was some kind of 'scarlet woman', snatching him away from his long-term girlfriend. I hope very much indeed too that we can be friends."

They walked back to the gallery together and said goodbye. Then both, simultaneously, leant forward and hugged each other.

"Goodbye Sam, I hope to see you soon." Nadia said. Then she turned and walked away.

Sam gazed after her, gratitude and relief for Nadia's kindness and understanding flooding through her. She hoped they could be friends, true friends.

Then she turned and went back into the gallery to get on with her work.

**

Sam could only hope that Federico's mother was in the same frame of mind as Nadia but she doubted it.

She lay awake the night before they were due to meet her again. She was sleepless with anxiety. If it all went badly, if she was resented as the woman who ruined all her plans, how would she be able to live with a mother-in-law who disliked her, who hated her for stealing her son away from the girl she had plans for him to marry?

She dressed carefully in the smartest but most demure dress she owned, anxious not to give a bad impression from the start. The day was going to be difficult enough without her looking like a temptress.

He picked her up at eleven. He kissed her and said. "Don't worry. It will be alright," but Sam wasn't sure that even he believed what he was saying.

The grand Palladian villa was on the outskirts of Naples in the neighbourhood of Chiaia. They drove along the waterfront park, the largest green space in the city, lined with enormous houses situated behind ornate gates.

Sam, if it were possible, became even more nervous. She knew Federico's family was wealthy, but it was obvious that they were talking millionaire status, not just reasonably well-off.

They stopped at last and the gates opened automatically as they drove towards them. Large gardens stretched down towards the sea and Sam could see at least two gardeners at work tending the flower beds and the already immaculate lawn. The view was stunning and she tried not to gasp. "I didn't realise…" she began.

"Having money doesn't necessarily make you happier," he said, trying to reassure her.

She was tempted to reply. "But it helps," but wisely held her tongue.

She felt very much out of her depth. They passed a dovecote with white fluttering birds and then a series of

235

garages with someone she assumed was the chauffeur cleaning a pair of Alpha Romeos. Federico's father had certainly made some money after his humble beginnings in the village. Or had he married money? Was that why Federico's mother had such an air of entitlement about her? Of course, his stepfather Piero had money too.

They drew up at the porticoed front door of the mansion.

His mother came to meet them as they got out of the car.

She came towards Sam and kissed her coolly on both cheeks. "Welcome," she said, but Sam could discern no warmth in her tone.

After she had greeted her son she said, "I thought we would have lunch on the terrace."

"Good idea," Federico said. He took hold of Sam's hand and guided her into the house. She was grateful for this gesture of solidarity. He could easily have left her and walked with his mother as she no doubt expected.

They entered the wide hallway and Sam gazed up at the beautifully frescoed ceiling.

"*Sixteenth century*," Federico's mother remarked, her eyes following Sam's gaze. "Of course, you are an artist. You will appreciate these things."

They went through what seemed like a series of opulent rooms lined with antique furniture and white sofas. Sam couldn't help thinking that they had obviously never had muddy children bouncing on them. Then they were out on the terrace overlooking that wonderful bay. The table was laid for four with crystal glasses and fine bone china but they first moved to other chairs further along for a glass of freshly squeezed lemon juice tinkling with ice and served by a maid in uniform.

She couldn't help but mentally compare it to the bustling friendly kitchen table of Giulia's house with the boys joshing and pulling each other's legs and the happy family atmosphere, even the apartment over the gallery with Gianfranco tunelessly singing opera while he cooked with Richard fondly looking on.

Poor Frederico, she thought. How had he survived such a frigid childhood? No wonder he had been conditioned to obey his mother's every wish.

His stepfather appeared and once again kissed her hand. They moved to the dining table. The food was exquisite, no doubt cooked by a chef in the kitchen.

Conversation was stilted. Federico's mother asked her about her family. It felt more like a job interview than a conversation. Sam couldn't help wondering if she was trying to gauge if her parents had money, if they were 'something' in the local community. If her son was marrying beneath him in social standing.

Federico was very quiet.

The whole thing was torture and she struggled to eat anything.

"Is it not to your liking?" His mother enquired.

"No, no, it's not that. It is all delicious. It's just that it is very hot and I find it hard to eat when it's warm."

The meal was over at last and Federico's mother said "Come Sam. You and I will walk around the garden and we will leave the men to talk."

It was issued in a tone of command rather than a request.

Sam got hurriedly to her feet, not daring to look at Federico. This was it. She would be warned to give him up in no uncertain terms.

Not that she would of course.

They walked together down the steps. They moved in silence for a while, Sam trying to fall into step with the other woman. The garden was beautiful and the scent of roses was overwhelming.

"I love this garden," Federico's mother said suddenly in a more friendly tone.

"It is very beautiful," Sam agreed. She buried her nose in a gardenia.

"Those are my pride and joy," his mother said.

"I would love to paint this view." Sam said.

"I hope you will. Federico has shown me some of your paintings. He is very proud of you."

"It's very kind of you to say so."

"I was quite good at art and I would have loved to go to art school, but I wasn't allowed." Her tone was quite wistful.

"But you could still paint if you wanted to," Sam remarked.

"Yes, I could, you are right. I have never done so because I was discouraged when I was young. Maybe you could help me. Show me how you get perspective, all of that."

"I would love to," Sam replied.

She realised with surprise and pleasure that the other woman was smiling at her.

"Sam, Samantha. I think we must talk. I think we must, how do you say in English? 'Clear the air?' Federico has explained the situation to you. Nadia's parents were our dearest friends and her father was his father's best friend from university. The children always got on so well and Nadia's mother and I always joked that they would marry. Then as they grew the idea seemed to become firmly fixed in our

238

minds that they would end up together. We just took it for granted. Then you came along and I could see Federico struggling. You may think that I am cold and unfeeling but I do love my son very much and I knew he had strong feelings for you and he was trying to come to terms with what we had led him to believe were our expectations, even his duty, if you like, to marry Nadia. But in the end, it is my son's happiness which is the most important thing and I am ashamed that I seem to have been putting such pressure on him. It has been helped by Nadia coming to me and explaining that she too was struggling with the weight of expectation and that she wanted to be free as well to make her own choice. I have talked to her mother and she and I have both realised how foolish we have been, forcing our wishes on our children. You are Federico's choice and I respect him for it. If I have seemed overbearing and unsympathetic I apologise. He is an honourable person and was struggling to do the right thing."

"I know he was. At first, I thought he was just playing with me and I was furious. Then I realised he was worried he was letting Nadia, you and everyone down. Thank you for saying what you have just said. I was so worried you wouldn't like me, would resent me and that it would make life difficult."

"So, we can be friends?"

Tears were in Sam's eyes. "Oh thank you. Thank you so much. Yes please."

"Shall we go back and join the men? I think Federico will be wondering what we are talking about and getting anxious."

She suddenly leant forward and took Sam in a warm embrace. "Welcome to the family Sam. I think you will be a very valuable addition and you will be very good for Federico.

239

I can see that you know what is important in this life and it is not all this," she waved her hand around at the enormous house and garden, "but it is love and affection which is at the core of living a good life."

"Although all this is very lovely too." Sam laughed and the other woman laughed as well. They were still laughing as they arrived back at the house, arm in arm.

Federico's face was a picture as he saw them arrive and he half rose from his seat as they came towards him.

"You have a real treasure here," Federico's mother said.

"Mamma, you don't need to tell me that. I knew she was from the first moment she started shouting at me."

"Shouting at you?" Her expression was one of puzzlement.

"Ah mamma, I don't think I ever told you how we first met," he said, taking Sam's hand and beginning to tell the tale.

Chapter 35

Giulia looked absolutely radiant.

She was wearing a dress handed down through generations of her family, antique lace over a shining satin bodice and skirt in a creamy colour that set off her auburn hair to perfection. In her hair, her mother had arranged tiny cream roses. The bouquet, paid for and given to her by Alberto, as was the tradition, also consisted of cream roses.

Sam was wearing a long turquoise dress and the brothers, looking very uncomfortable, were in smart suits with crisp white shirts and matching turquoise ties. Sam knew that the moment the day was over they would be back in their t-shirts and jeans.

Giulia, Maria and Sam came out of the bedroom to be greeted by the menfolk. Enrico took one look at his daughter and promptly burst into uncontrollable sobs. Maria went to stroke his back to console him.

"My Enrico. He has always been so sentimental. He is overwhelmed at the sight of his daughter and also the fact that she will no longer be part of the family, but living with Alberto in Naples."

"I will not be too far away, Papa," Giulia soothed him, "and I will visit often."

"And the bambini," her mother said, "when they come, we will be able to look after them here in the village."

"Hey mamma, not so fast." Giulia laughed, "Let me get married first."

She turned to her father "Ready, Papa?"

Her father had wiped his face. "Si, cara mia."

The door opened and they passed through, past the huge white bow tied to the door knocker which told everyone that a wedding was taking place, and out onto the front step.

Sam was amazed. It seemed that the whole village was gathered in the street outside, with people hanging out over balconies as well. There was a storm of clapping and cheering as the bride appeared. Sam recognised many of them, old aunts and uncles and cousins, neighbours and friends. Amongst the crowd, she could see Federico's mother Olivia and Piero his stepfather. The acceptance of Sam and the welcome Olivia had given her had brought unexpected benefits because Maria and Enrico, anxious to let bygones be bygones, had invited them to the wedding. Olivia and Maria had had a long and tearful conversation during which Olivia had apologised sincerely for cutting Maria's brother off from his family, realising she had been thoughtless and unkind. Olivia explained that she had been so distraught when her husband had been ill and then died, she hadn't given a thought to Maria's feelings. Maria being Maria, had hugged her and said there was nothing to forgive and she knew Olivia had loved her brother deeply which was the important thing, so the two had reconciled.

There too was little Alfredo gripping his grandfather's hand. Even Nonna Irene, Giulia's great-grandmother, had been brought out into the sunshine and was sitting in a chair in front of the neighbouring house. She was too frail to attend the wedding, but Giulia went across and kissed her before she turned and joined her father once more for the long journey up to the church. Excited children ran alongside them as the small procession made its way to the top of the steps.

There Alberto was waiting for her, with his family. Sam was gratified to see that he gave a small gasp of pleasure at the sight of his bride. She saw the look that passed between them, one of pure love and she could not be but exceedingly happy for her friend. There was no doubt they adored each other.

Alberto walked with his mother behind Giulia and her father. Sam thought what a lovely Italian custom that was, that the bridegroom's mother entered the church with him. Everyone else walked behind them in a long crocodile and the procession of friends and family wound its way up the steep steps to the church at the top of the hill where more people were waiting to cheer and clap as the bridal party appeared. Everyone stood outside the church as the bride and groom with their parents walked in first, unlike at an English wedding, and the congregation followed with much bustling and hurrying to get the best seats. The priest was waiting to receive the happy couple and Giulia handed Sam her bouquet. Sam sat with Maria, Enrico and the brothers in the front pew. Maria ready with a large clean hanky to hand to her husband who was already crying again.

The mass began and Alberto and Giulia knelt at the altar. At the end of the mass, they began to take their vows and Sam suddenly felt a pressure on her arm. She half turned and Federico was sitting directly behind her. He reached for her hand and she grasped it and held it firmly while the vows were said. There could be no more explicit expression of intent than this, she thought happily, overwhelmed with emotion.

Finally, the bride and groom exited the church to a shower of rice and rose petals and they all proceeded down to the small hotel in the valley accompanied by more clapping and cheering and small children scrabbling for the coins thrown by the bridal party…

Sam had been to quite a few weddings in England, some quite formal, others quite relaxed including one in a field, but she had never been to a wedding quite like this where the whole community seemed to participate. She knew this was where she wanted to be married too and her parents were already excited at the thought of the celebrations to come.

The noise at the wedding breakfast was deafening. Every few minutes someone would stand up and announce a 'Brindisi', a toast to the happy couple and there would be a roar as they all raised their glasses and banged their hands on the tables. Enrico, still overcome with emotion, stood to make his speech, mopping his face frequently with the endless supply of hankies Maria seemed to have in her capacious handbag. Sam couldn't help but think that was a sign of true love when you knew the exact moment to hand your husband a hanky for his tears.

As the wine flowed the cheers got more raucous and culminated with the bride lifting her wedding dress demurely and removing the special garter of roses she wore on her leg. She tossed it into the assembled throng where all the young men scrambled for it. The victor, her brother Giovanni, wore it on his head while standing on the table and the cheers and whistles grew, if it were possible, even louder.

"Baci, baci," yelled the assembled crowd with more table thumping and the bride and groom obliged by giving each other a lingering kiss.

Then the dancing began, at first a slow dance led by Giulia and Alberto, followed by all the guests. Slow dances led to the tarantella, everyone holding hands in a circle and whirling around to the music, then reversing direction.

The music went on late into the evening. Richard danced a slow dance with Sam and whispered, "Next time, it will be you."

"I hope so," Sam whispered back, looking over and smiling at Federico who was watching her and waiting impatiently for his turn to dance with her.

Then at last the bonbonniere were handed, those little tokens of sugared almonds tied in small lace bags with a cream rose. A slip of paper inside bore the names 'Giulia and Alberto'.

Federico, holding Sam close on the dance floor, explained that they traditionally meant wealth, health, long life and happiness but the cynics said they were the bitter sweet of marriage with the sugar on the outside and the bitter almonds inside.

They laughed, "Ours won't be like that though will it?" They said to each other with certainty as they gazed at each other through a haze of love.

"Just the sweet and the long life of health and happiness. I don't care about the wealth." Sam added.

Giulia threw her bouquet. Her aim was excellent and Sam caught it with ease. They grinned at each other.

After Giulia and Alberto had left for their honeymoon, they wandered outside. The stars were bright in a clear night sky and the moon was full.

She was in the arms of the man she loved and who loved her, in a place she loved.

So, everything was perfect. Absolutely perfect.